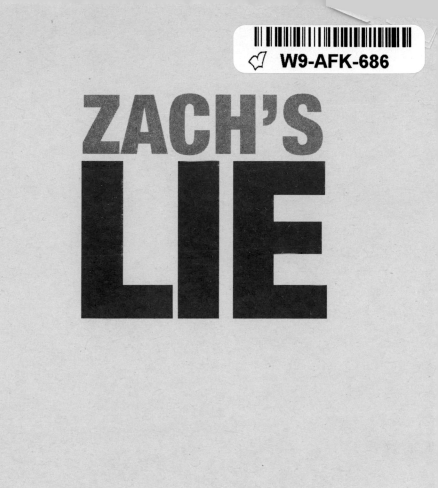
ZACH'S LIE

Other Novels by Roland Smith

Thunder Cave

Jaguar

Sasquatch

The Last Lobo

ZACH'S LIE

roland smith

Hyperion Paperbacks for Children
New York

First Hyperion Paperback edition, 2003
17 19 20 18
Printed in the United States of America

Library of Congress Cataloging-in-Publication Data
Smith, Roland, 1951–
Zach's Lie / Roland Smith.— 1st ed.
p.   cm.
Summary: When Jack Osborne is befriended by his school's custodian
and a Basque girl, he begins to adjust to his family's sudden move to
Elko, Nevada, after entering the Witness Security Program, but the drug cartel
against which his father will testify is determined to track them down.
ISBN 0-7868-0617-6 (trade hc) ISBN 0-7868-1440-3 (paperback)
[1. Witness—Protection—Fiction. 2. Narcotics dealers—Fiction.
3. Basques—Fiction. 4. Nevada—Fiction.] I. Title.

PZ7.S65766 Zac 2001
[Fic]—dc21   00-59725

Visit www.hyperionchildrensbooks.com

V475-2873-0 14017

*This one is for my nephew
Zachary Teters, a great reader,
and an extraordinary young man*

Part One

FLIGHT

Friday, August 25

Commander IF is in my shirt pocket.

We are sitting on an airplane in the last row. Five people—my sister, my mother, Aunt Doris, and Uncle Don.

We got on the airplane before the other passengers. "Too risky to board through the gate," Uncle Don had explained. Airport security led us through the cargo area underneath the airport. This must have all been prearranged, because no one blinked an eye as we wove our way through the maze of baggage conveyor belts. When we got on board, the flight attendants looked at us with curiosity, but they didn't ask us why we rated this kind of treatment. I guess they knew better.

"We'll be boarding the other passengers in a few minutes," one of the attendants said, and showed us to our seats.

Aunt Doris and Uncle Don took the aisle seats. Mom sat next to my sister on Aunt Doris's side. I took the window seat on Uncle

Don's side. Mom has a book to read, my sister has a pile of movie magazines, and I have my journal and pencil.

Aunt Doris and Uncle Don do not have anything to read. They are working. Aunt Doris has her head turned and is watching the flight attendants behind us put away cans of pop and juice. Uncle Don stares straight ahead.

"Here they come," Uncle Don says.

The other passengers start making their way down the aisle, finding their seats, stuffing bags into the overhead compartments. The five of us stare at the passengers' faces, wondering if any of them know. . . .

Commander IF had come to Jack Osborne when he was nine years old, just after his caped-crusader days.

Jack wasn't proud of this, but on windy nights he used to slip into his sister's red leotards, safety-pin a sheet around his neck, lean out his bedroom window with his arms stretched, and pretend to fly like the superheroes he watched on television. This had come to an end the night he leaned out a little too far and discovered he could not fly, falling through his father's grape arbor and snapping the thick gnarled vines that were said to have come from cuttings grown by President Thomas Jefferson at Monticello in 1804.

Hearing the crash, Jack's father, Neil Osborne, ran outside in his boxer shorts and beamed the flashlight on his crumpled son, who was covered in red scratches and purple grape juice. He then shone the light up through the gaping hole in the arbor, took a deep breath, and slowly let it out through flared nostrils.

4

Jack's mother, Patricia Osborne, called down from the bedroom window, "Is everything okay?"

Mr. Osborne looked up and said, "It's just another one of those darn caped crusaders. He must have stalled in the storm."

"Do I need to call nine-one-one?"

Mr. Osborne looked down at his only son. Jack had been to the hospital so many times for stitches and broken bones that his father had considered buying him a permanent room there.

"Is anything broken, Jacko?"

"I think my leg," Jack said through gritted teeth.

Mr. Osborne bent down with the flashlight and looked at Jack's leg. "They're going to get a big kick out of these red leotards in the emergency room."

As it turned out, both legs were broken, and Jack spent the next six weeks wired to a hospital bed with enough screws and pins in his legs to set off metal detectors for the rest of his life.

The third day that Jack was in the hospital his father brought him a wooden model of the space shuttle, which he had carved in his woodworking shop. Mr. Osborne was always doing something with his hands. Building, carving, sketching, fixing, driving, writing, flying—Jack's earliest memories were of his father's busy and clever hands.

The next day, as Jack was practicing space shuttle landings on his cast in his hospital bed, he discovered that the cockpit opened and inside was a tiny astronaut. He named the astronaut Commander Jacko—at first.

Commander Jacko had been a Navy fighter pilot as

Jack's father had been before he married Jack's mother. He looked a lot like Jack's father when he was young, although at two inches tall Commander Jacko was quite a bit shorter than Neil Osborne.

Jack changed the astronaut's name the day his father caught Jack talking to him in the hospital room.

His father heard Jack jabbering away from down the hallway. He came into Jack's room expecting to see his wife or a nurse, but Jack was alone. He was lying on the bed with both legs in casts, an I.V. tube attached to his arm, and the space shuttle with the tiny astronaut resting on his chest.

"Who were you talking to, Jacko?"

Jack stared at his father as if he didn't understand, but he knew perfectly well what his father was asking.

Mr. Osborne sat down on the bed and picked up the space shuttle. "I sure wanted to fly one of these babies."

Jack knew this. Everyone knew this. His father had come very close to becoming a shuttle pilot. Jack wasn't sure what had gotten in his way, but it had something to do with some trouble that he had gotten into when he was a combat pilot during the Gulf War.

"You know," his father said, "when I was your age I had an imaginary friend too."

Jack still didn't let on that he knew what his father was talking about.

"Yep," his father continued. "My friend was a scuba diver and I spent hours chatting away with him. One day your grandfather caught me. He told me he used to have a friend too when he was a boy. His friend's name was Mr. IF."

"Funny name," Jack commented.

6

"It stood for Imaginary Friend. Do you know what your grandfather told me?"

Jack shook his head.

"He said I should enjoy my imaginary friend for as long as I could, because one day Mr. IF was going to leave and I would never have another friend like him. My imaginary friend left when we were vacationing at the beach. I was building sand castles and Mr. IF said he had a secret mission. He walked into the surf wearing his scuba gear and I never saw him again."

Jack's imaginary friend took off for Mars when Jack was eleven years old and he didn't see him for two years.

Commander IF returned the morning Jack was packing his things to be moved to their new home. The Osbornes couldn't take everything with them because the house they were moving into was smaller than the house they were moving out of. "Considerably smaller," Uncle Don had warned them. The Osbornes had to choose what they would take, which wasn't a big deal for Jack because most of the things he cared about were small. This was not the case for his mother and sister. They were attached to big things, many of which had to be left behind.

Jack was sorting through his stuff, deciding what he would take with him, and found the space shuttle in the bottom of a box in his closet. The shuttle looked like it had been to Mars and back. Jack flew the shuttle from the closet, made a perfect landing on his bed, and Commander IF stepped out of the cockpit again.

"You got back just in time," Jack told him. "We're moving."

I know, Commander IF said.

Jack put Commander IF in his shirt pocket.

With his caped-crusader days behind him, Jack had to find something to fill the void. Before he left the hospital he discovered two things. The first was books. His mother brought him stacks of them. *Treasure Island*, *Tarzan*, *Sherlock Holmes*— he began to read like he had never read before and he continued to do so after he got out of the hospital.

The second thing Jack had discovered was journal writing. While Jack read, his father would sometimes sit beside his bed writing and sketching in a beautiful journal he had picked up during one of his trips.

"What are you writing?" Jack asked him one night.

"Just some thoughts. How's the book?"

"Good." Jack paused. "I wouldn't mind having a journal like that for my thoughts."

"I think that can be arranged," his father said.

A week later his father gave him five blank journals. Jack had managed to fill up one journal every year since his accident. As he sat on the airplane with the fifth journal in his lap, he wondered where he was going to get a new journal when this one was filled.

"Our flying time to Salt Lake City will be two hours and fifty minutes," the pilot announced over the intercom.

This was the first hint Jack had heard about where they were going. His mother knew. Uncle Don and Aunt Doris knew. But Jack and his sister did not know—-or so she swore to him, but Jack suspected his mother had told her.

"Will that be our final destination?" Jack asked Uncle Don.

"No."

"Are we catching a connecting flight in Salt Lake?"

"Just relax, Zach," Uncle Don said.

Zach. Jack was still not used to hearing that name directed toward him. They had chosen the name *Zach* because it sounded like "Jack." "In case you slip up," Uncle Don had told him. "You can claim you said 'Zach,' not 'Jack.'"

His sister had gotten to pick her own name. She had chosen the name Wanda, which did not sound anything like her real name, Joanne. Jack complained that it wasn't fair that she got to pick her name and he didn't. "Wanda is older than you, Zach," Aunt Doris explained. "She is less likely to slip up."

His mother, who had renamed herself Mary, sided with Aunt Doris. Pointing out that Jack hadn't picked out the name *Jack*, either. "Your father named you," she said.

"If anyone *slips up* it will be Wanda, not me," Jack had said, defending himself.

Actually, he didn't mind being called Zach, but he would have felt better about it if he had chosen the name himself.

The airplane pushed back from the terminal and began taxiing toward the runway. The last time Jack had flown, he sat in the jump seat behind his father in the cockpit. Not today, Jack thought, not ever again. The Osbornes were the Grangers now. Zach Granger looked in his shirt pocket. Commander IF was nodding in agreement.

As the airplane took off, Zach began to read through the brief journal entries of the past month. There were only two.

Monday, July 24

Men broke into our house last night. I'm racking my brain wondering if there is anything I could have done to stop them. Where was the caped crusader when I needed him?

Dad would have done something if he had been there. But they're saying that he's the reason the men came into the house. . . .

Jack had been sound asleep when the man clamped his hand over Jack's mouth.

"Make one sound and you will die," the man whispered. To prove the seriousness of his words, he held the point of his knife an inch from Jack's right eye. Jack wet himself. The man was dressed in dark clothes. He wore a ski mask over his head and surgical gloves on his hands. "Turn over on your stomach."

Jack did as he was told. His arms were wrenched behind his back. He heard tape being torn. His wrists were bound together, then the man flipped him back over and slapped a wide piece of tape over his mouth. Jack felt a mixture of terror, anger, and shame at his helplessness. His stomach heaved.

"None of that," the man hissed, sitting him up. "Breathe through your nose. Deep breaths."

Jack tried, but found it very difficult because he was shivering uncontrollably.

"Stand up. We are going downstairs."

Jack swung his legs out of bed, but they were shaking so badly he couldn't stand. Where were his mother and sister? The man jerked him to his feet and half dragged him down the stairs. His mother and sister were sitting on the sofa in the living room, both of them bound and gagged. The man pushed Jack onto the sofa next to his mother. The only light in the room came from the small lamp on the end table. Three men with ski masks stood off in the shadows looking at them silently. After what seemed like a very long time, one of the men stepped forward with a cell phone in one hand and a gun in the other. He knelt in front of Mrs. Osborne.

"In a moment this phone will ring," he spoke very deliberately as if he were reading from a prepared script. "I will answer it." He pointed the gun at Joanne's head. She began sobbing. He ignored her. "I am going to remove the tape from your mouth, Mrs. Osborne. When I do you are not to say a word. Do you understand?"

She nodded. With a quick movement, he tore the tape off. Mrs. Osborne winced in pain, but she did not cry out.

"After I answer the phone I will hold it to your ear and you are to say, 'They will kill us if you talk.' Nothing more. Say it now."

11

"They will . . ." She could not seem to get the words out.

"Get her a glass of water," the man ordered.

One of the other men walked into the kitchen. He did not turn the light on. Jack heard the cupboard open and water running in the sink. When he returned with the water, the man with the pistol held the glass to Mrs. Osborne's lips without moving the gun away from Joanne's head. Some of the water dribbled onto Mrs. Osborne's nightgown.

"Better?" the man asked. Mrs. Osborne nodded. "Good. 'They will kill us if you talk.' Repeat the words."

"They will kill us if you talk." The words were shaky but clear.

"Now we will wait," he said, still pointing the gun at Joanne's head.

The Osbornes jumped when the phone finally rang. The man let it ring three times before flipping it open and holding it to his ear. He listened for a moment, then held the phone to Mrs. Osborne's ear.

They heard Neil Osborne shouting through the tiny speaker. "Patricia? Is that you? Patricia? Are the kids there? Are you all right?"

The man cocked the gun.

Patricia Osborne closed her eyes tightly. "They will kill us if you talk," she said quickly.

The man flipped the phone closed.

"What now?" she asked.

"We will wait." He backed into the shadows.

"Who are—"

A man came up behind her and put a fresh strip of tape over her mouth.

The Osbornes did not know how long they waited. The men stood silently in the shadows. The phone rang. The man flipped it open. Once again he listened, then flipped it closed. He whispered something to the man who had brought the water. The man went back into the kitchen and returned with the white timer Mrs. Osborne used for cooking.

"We will be leaving you in a few moments," the man with the gun said. "Before we do I wish to make something clear." He paused, looking directly at Mrs. Osborne. "We are very serious men. If you call the police or tell anyone about what happened this evening we will come back and kill you and your children. We will also kill your husband. You have my word on this. There is no place you can hide if you break my trust. I will find you wherever you go. Do you understand?"

She nodded.

"Good. Remain quiet and this will become nothing more than an unpleasant memory for you." The man who had gone to the kitchen handed him the timer. "We will leave now, but before we do we will free the boy's hands. You will remain where you are without moving for one half-hour. We will be watching."

He stepped back into the light and put the timer on the floor in front of Jack. "When this rings you may free your mother and sister, but not one second before. Do you understand?"

Jack nodded. A man came up behind him, pushed Jack forward, and cut the tape around his wrists. Then the men left the house. They heard a car start in the driveway and back out. Jack looked at his mother. She shook her head vigorously and nodded at the timer.

Jack tried to rub some feeling back into his hands. He reached up to take the tape off his mouth, but his mother and sister shook their heads no and stamped their feet on the rug. The man hadn't said to leave his gag on, but he waited. When the timer finally rang, Jack ran into the kitchen and found a pair of scissors. He cut his mother free first, then Joanne. A moment later they were all holding each other and crying.

"What's happening, Mom?" Joanne asked over and over again.

"What about Dad?" Jack sobbed.

"I don't know," Patricia Osborne said. "I don't know."

They took showers, then sat at the kitchen table in their bathrobes trying to figure out what had happened. The most logical explanation was that Neil Osborne had been kidnapped. He spent a lot of time in Central and South America doing business and kidnappings were not uncommon there. Mrs. Osborne was certain that the next step would be a ransom demand, but she was afraid that Neil would try something heroic and get himself killed before she could gather the money to pay them.

During the Gulf War, Neil had gotten into trouble for refusing to leave a downed pilot on the ground. He circled the area until the rescue helicopter arrived. On his way back to base, his jet ran out of fuel and he had to ditch it in the Persian Gulf.

They sat at the table until dawn, and that's where the police found them when they stormed into the house.

The back and front doors were kicked in at the exact same moment.

"Police!"

"Freeze!"

"Keep your hands on the table!"

Armed men and women wearing black jump suits, flak vests, and helmets swarmed into the kitchen, handcuffing the Osbornes before they could stand up from the kitchen table.

"House is secure," a radio crackled.

Two men came into the kitchen wearing gray suits. "Patricia Osborne?" one of the men asked.

She nodded.

"DEA," he said. "Federal Drug Enforcement Agency. I'm Agent Pelton and this is Agent Dayton. We have a warrant authorizing us to arrest your house and all of its contents."

They're arresting our *house*? Jack thought.

Agent Pelton sat down at the table.

"Are *we* under arrest?" Mrs. Osborne demanded. She'd had just about enough.

"Technically, no."

"Then why have you handcuffed my children?" she shouted.

Agent Pelton did not react to her angry outburst. "It's really for your own protection, Mrs. Osborne," he explained calmly. "And our officers', of course. Most folks tend to react negatively to having their homes ransacked. I know I would if it were mine. I can have the cuffs removed if you promise not to interfere with our activities."

Mrs. Osborne took a deep breath to try to calm herself. "We won't interfere."

15

Agent Dayton unlocked their cuffs. It sounded like a troop of mountain gorillas were tearing their house apart. Two men came into the kitchen and began dumping drawers of silverware into cardboard boxes. Jack wondered how a spoon could break the law.

"Maybe we should go into the living room," Agent Pelton said. "It might be quieter."

The living room was quieter, but not much. "Why don't you all sit on the sofa and relax," Agent Pelton suggested.

The Osbornes looked at the sofa. Before the police burst in they had decided to get rid of the sofa. "We'll stand," Mrs. Osborne said. They watched as a parade of men and women flowed in and out of the front door like ants. They came in empty-handed and left with their arms filled with the Osbornes' possessions. Parked in front of the house were two big moving trucks surrounded by flashing police cars. The front yard was cordoned off with yellow tape stenciled with the words: CRIME SCENE. Standing beyond the tape were several neighbors, two of whom were being interviewed by local television news stations.

"What's this all about?" Mrs. Osborne asked, with a great deal more calm than she felt. "What do we have to do with the DEA?"

"All I can tell you, Mrs. Osborne, is that your husband has been arrested."

"He's alive?"

The question momentarily threw Agent Pelton. "Of course he's alive."

"Thank God!" Mrs. Osborne covered her face with her hands and began sobbing.

"Your husband is currently in Federal custody," Agent Pelton went on.

"Where is he?" Jack asked.

"Brownsville, Texas, but we'll be transporting him to this jurisdiction later today. Is there a reason you thought he was dead?"

"No," Mrs. Osborne spoke quickly. "We haven't heard from him and we were worried."

"It would be best if you told me the truth, Mrs. Osborne."

"That is the truth," she insisted. "Why is he in custody?"

A man came over and told Agent Pelton that they needed him in the kitchen.

"Excuse me," Agent Pelton said.

"What's going on, Mom?" Joanne asked.

"I don't know."

"What does Dad have to do with drugs?" Jack asked.

"Nothing!" Mrs. Osborne said. "I mean I don't know. Listen—" she lowered her voice. "We need to stay calm. I'm sure it's all a big mistake."

"Maybe we should call an attorney," Jack whispered.

Agent Pelton came back into the living room.

"I want to call my attorney," Mrs. Osborne said in her calmest voice.

"No problem, but before you do can you explain this?" He held up a plastic evidence bag. Inside the bag were wadded strips of duct tape.

"Duct tape," Mrs. Osborne shrugged as if it were the most normal thing in the world.

"I know what it is. Where did it come from?"

"The garbage can underneath the kitchen sink."

"That's not what I meant."

"I used some tape to seal a box I mailed out."

"Right. Then where's the spool? It wasn't in the kitchen."

"I don't know. I might have used it all up."

"Then where's the empty spool? It wasn't in the garbage can."

"I have no idea."

"Right." Agent Pelton looked at Jack. "Jack, isn't it?"

Jack nodded.

"Can I see your hands, son?"

Jack glanced at his mother. She nodded for him to go ahead. He held them out. Agent Pelton looked carefully at Jack's wrists and forearms. "Have you been shaving your arms, son?"

Jack shook his head, wondering what Agent Pelton was talking about.

"You seem to be missing a lot of black hair on your wrist," Agent Pelton pointed out. He held up the tape. "Oddly enough, there are a lot of black hairs stuck to this duct tape." He looked at Mrs. Osborne. "You weren't wrapping your son up, were you?" He walked over to the sofa. The white timer was still lying on the carpet. Agent Pelton pulled a plastic bag out of his pocket and put the timer into it.

"No matter what happens," Mrs. Osborne whispered, "don't say a word about last night."

Agent Pelton felt the sofa cushions, then sniffed his hands. "Do you have pets?"

Jack flushed bright red. He knew what Agent Pelton had smelled.

"No," Mrs. Osborne said.

"Okay, let's stop beating around the bush. How many were there?"

Mrs. Osborne looked him right in the eye. "I don't know what you're talking about."

"Did they threaten to kill you?"

Mrs. Osborne did not answer.

"The only way you'll be safe is with us. We can protect you, Mrs. Osborne. We can protect your children."

"I want to call my attorney."

"I'll get you a phone."

3

Mom called her and Dad's attorney, June Saunders, who has been a friend of the family since before they got married. She came over and talked with Agent Pelton for a few minutes, then told us to get dressed. June took us to a hotel and we checked into a double room under her name, and that's where I'm writing this.

"I want you all to go to bed," June told them. "What you need right now is sleep. While you're recovering, I'll try to find out what's going on. No one knows you're here and I want to keep it that way. If the phone rings, don't answer it. And for heaven's sake don't answer the door unless it's me. I don't want you talking to any reporters or the police for the time being."

"What about Neil?" Mrs. Osborne asked.

"I'll try to get in touch with him and let him know you're okay. Just go to sleep. That's the only priority right now. I'll bring back some takeout."

June returned about four o'clock in the afternoon with

Chinese food. The Osbornes looked a little better after a few hours' rest. Jack started opening the cartons of food as soon as they hit the table. Joanne sat in a chair staring numbly out the window. Patricia, who had just stepped out of the shower was brushing her hair.

"Is there someplace we can talk privately?" June asked.

"This concerns Jack and Joanne as much as it concerns me," Patricia said firmly.

"You're the boss." June put her briefcase on the coffee table.

"What have you found out?"

"A lot," June grimaced. "And none of it's good. I had a long conversation with Agent Pelton, who seems like a pretty decent guy. He said that he would give us more information after you consent to an interview. I've tentatively scheduled it for tomorrow morning."

Patricia put her hand up. "I haven't decided if I'm going to talk to him or not."

"You might not have a choice, but we can get into that later."

"Just tell me what's going on."

June opened her briefcase and took out a yellow legal pad filled with notes. "I'll start with Neil. I wasn't able to speak to him, but I did get in touch with his attorney."

"His attorney?" Patricia repeated. "I thought you were his attorney."

"Not anymore. He's retained the services of Benjamin Bender. He is a very expensive and well-known criminal defense attorney, who, by the way, suggested that you talk to him before you talk to me. I told him that I would pass that on before we got into any details here."

"What's that mean?"

"We have a couple ways that we can go, Patricia. I can advise you as your friend or I can advise you as your attorney. Either way is fine with me. Mr. Bender wants to represent you and Neil. He said that Neil requested it, but you can hire whoever you want to represent you. It's your call."

"I want you as my attorney."

"I'm not a criminal attorney," June began. "It might be best—"

"We're not criminals!" Patricia snapped.

"Okay, okay. Sit down." June motioned her into a chair. "I know you've been through a lot, but you need to stay calm. Let me tell you what I know."

She explained that Neil Osborne had been arrested for drug trafficking. He was being held in the Federal Detention Center downtown. "Their case is pretty solid. They have photographs, videos, phone conversations. They've been on his trail for over a year."

"A year? That doesn't seem possible. How could Neil—"

"You told me yourself that you haven't seen Neil for more than two weeks in the past four months." June looked at Joanne and Jack uncomfortably. "That since he bought the airline company he's been pretty scarce around the house."

When Jack's father had left the Navy, he became a commercial airline pilot. The job paid well. It had bought them a big house in the suburbs, nice cars, good clothes, and great vacations. But after five years Jack's father got fed up with flying "busloads" of irritable passengers over the same boring routes. When Jack fell out the window, his father took a long leave of absence to consider his options. He decided to buy a small airline company based in Texas and began flying cargo into Mexico and Central and South America. Since he had bought the company, he had been away more often than at home. And when he was home, it seemed to Jack and Joanne that all their parents did was argue. The arguments had gotten so bad during the past year that Jack and Joanne were worried that their parents would split up.

Patricia pounded the table with her fists. "I just don't understand how he could get himself into something like this without my knowing anything about it!"

June reached over and took her hands. "You'll have plenty of time to think about that later. Right now we have to figure out how to get you out of this mess."

"What's going to happen to him?"

"Are you sure you want me to talk about this right now?" She glanced at the kids again.

"Yes."

"Well, if half of what they appear to have on Neil turns out to be true, they could lock him up and throw away the key."

Mrs. Osborne covered her face with her hands and began crying. Joanne and June put their arms around her and joined in. Jack had thought that the men coming into their house was the most awful thing that had ever happened to him. But seeing his mother like this was worse. After a while his mother got up and went into the bathroom. She came back out a few minutes later with her face washed and a determined look in her eyes.

"What does all this mean to us?" she asked.

"That's the big question," June answered. "Agent Pelton doesn't think you're involved, but he does think that these people are trying to get to Neil through you."

"What people?" Patricia asked. "What's he talking about?"

June stared at her for a long time without saying anything. "Agent Pelton is convinced that somebody came to your house last night and had a conversation with you. Is there any truth to that?"

"No."

June took her hand again. "You can't do this on your own, Patricia. You've got to think of—"

There was a knock on the door. June walked over and looked through the peephole. "It's Benjamin Bender. I've seen him on talk shows. I guess he didn't trust me to pass his request on to you."

"Should we let him in?" Patricia asked.

June shrugged. "I don't see why not. But watch what you say. I'll jump in if I think he's getting into sensitive areas." She opened the door.

Benjamin Bender strode into the room as if he owned it, walking right past June Saunders to Patricia. "Mrs. Osborne? My name is Benjamin Bender." He wore a three-piece, charcoal gray, pinstriped suit and a starched white shirt with a yellow silk tie. His dark tan made his super-white teeth look like fresh snow. "Your husband has retained me to represent you."

"So I've heard." Patricia pointed to June. "This is my attorney, June Saunders."

24

"Ah, yes, Ms. Saunders. I believe we've spoken on the phone." He gave her a small nod then turned to Jack and Joanne. "And you must be Joanne! Your father said you were beautiful. He wasn't exaggerating."

Joanne rolled her eyes at Jack.

"And Jack," Bender continued. "You look a great deal like your father."

Jack did not like Mr. Benjamin Bender.

"How is Neil?" Patricia asked. "Have you seen him?"

"I just came from seeing him. He's doing fine under the circumstances. We'll straighten all this out, Mrs. Osborne. As usual, our Federal friends have gotten a little ahead of themselves and are abusing their powers."

"You mean Dad didn't do the things they told us?" Jack felt a glimmer of hope. Perhaps this was all a terrible mistake.

"Of course not!" Bender said vehemently. "He was just in the wrong place at the wrong time. Shall we sit down and discuss our options?"

When everyone was comfortable, Benjamin Bender opened his briefcase. "Before we begin I have a few questions. What did they take from your house?"

"I have no idea," Patricia said. "We left before they were finished."

"Computers?"

"Yes, I think so. Like I said, I don't know what they took."

"The house has been stripped," June broke in. "I was over there this afternoon. They left some of your personal things. Clothes, books, CDs, toys, some furniture, things like that, but everything else is gone."

Jack wondered if they had found the Jack in the Box. He hoped not.

"We will get all of your possessions back, eventually," Bender reassured them. "They just do this to harass people. Tell me, did your husband do any of his business from home?"

"Some," Patricia answered. "He has, or had, a home office where he worked when he was in town."

"I see. Did they—"

"Who really hired you, Mr. Bender?" June interrupted.

He turned to her as if he had never seen her before. "As I mentioned before, Neil Osborne hired me."

"When?"

"I don't see the relevance of that question."

"I think it's very relevant, Mr. Bender," Patricia said. "June has always been our attorney. Neil has never mentioned your name."

"I'm not surprised," Bender replied easily. "We were introduced just recently by a mutual friend."

"Who?"

"I'm not at liberty to say, but rest assured he's a good friend of Neil's and is very upset about this terrible injustice. My instructions are to spare no expense trying to help you and your husband." He quickly changed the subject. "Has the DEA attempted to interview you formally, Mrs. Osborne?"

"I told them I wanted to think about things for a while and speak with my attorney first."

"Very wise," Bender nodded in approval. "They will

insist on speaking with you, but I can delay them for several days."

"I'm scheduled to speak with them tomorrow morning."

"We can't have that," Bender scolded. "We have a lot of things to discuss before we grant the interview."

"I don't see how it can hurt," Patricia said. "I don't know anything about drugs."

Bender laughed. "That's beside the point, Mrs. Osborne. These people can trick you into saying things you don't really mean and that could get you and Neil into a great deal of trouble. My advice is to—"

"Mr. Bender," Patricia interrupted. "I have retained June Saunders as my attorney."

Bender's pleasant expression changed immediately. "Mrs. Osborne, you and your family are in serious trouble here. I am sure that Ms. Saunders is a good attorney and a good friend, but this situation is very complicated. Having separate representation is a mistake. As I told you, your husband's benefactor is very concerned about this situation. If anything unfortunate were to happen to you or your husband he would be very upset."

"What do you mean *unfortunate*?" June asked.

He continued to look at Patricia. "This is a potentially very dangerous situation we are dealing with here."

His words hung in the air for several seconds.

"You can represent my husband." Patricia was firm. "That's his choice. My choice, though, is to have June represent me."

"Perhaps Ms. Saunders and I can team up and represent you together."

"No."

"I see." Bender slowly closed his briefcase and stood up. "Does your husband know about this decision?"

"I haven't spoken with him since this happened."

"Well, perhaps you should before you make up your mind. I also suggest that you talk to him before you grant an interview to the authorities. He might be able to enlighten you further about his involvement in all of this. I would hate for you to jeopardize yourself or your family. We do not want to operate at cross purposes here and get tangled up. That is exactly what the DEA wants us to do and you are playing right into their hands by seeking separate representation."

"Thank you for your time, Mr. Bender." Patricia got up and opened the door for him.

"I do hope you change your mind, Mrs. Osborne. It would be best for everyone involved." He gave her a business card. "On the back is the number of my hotel. I'll be in town for a couple more days."

"One more thing before you leave," Patricia said.

"Certainly."

"How did you know where to find us? No one knows where we are. We aren't even registered under our own names."

The question seemed to throw Bender for a second, but he recovered quickly. "It wasn't that difficult, Mrs. Osborne."

Patricia closed the door behind him and turned to June. "If he could find us, they can find us."

"I think they already have," June said.

"I've got to talk to Neil."

"I'll call Agent Pelton."

Berry Jones and Paul Snider sat in a rental car a quarter mile away from the hotel watching the front entrance through a powerful spotting scope. The car was beginning to sour with the smell of hamburgers, coffee, and two large men who had not bathed in two days.

The men watched Benjamin Bender go in and come back out fifteen minutes later looking very unhappy. When June Saunders and the Osbornes finally came out, Berry and Paul followed them to the Federal Detention Center and discovered that they were not the only people following the Osbornes. Berry called Alonzo Aznar. "The cops are tailing them," he said.

"As I expected," Alonzo said. "Stick with them, but make sure you aren't spotted."

Alonzo hung up and looked out the small round window of the jet. He was the only passenger. The black sky was clear. City lights flickered thirty thousand feet below. He flipped the intercom switch and asked the pilot when they would be landing. A week earlier the pilot would have been Neil Osborne. Alonzo was going to miss Neil. He dialed another number.

Benjamin Bender answered the phone in his hotel room.

"So, how did it go?" Alonzo asked.

"Not very well," Bender told him. "Mrs. Osborne has retained her own attorney."

"I thought you would be more persuasive."

"She still might change her mind. I told her to talk to her

29

husband. He might be able to convince her."

"She is with him now." Alonzo raised his voice. "She might change *his* mind."

Bender was worried about this too, but didn't say so. "He seems to be with us on this thing, but he's worried about his family and what might happen to them."

"With good reason."

"He told me to tell you that if anything happened to them a certain document would be sent that would put an end to your operation."

Alonzo laughed. "Bold words from a pilot who knows virtually nothing about our operation."

"I wouldn't be so sure," Bender said. "He gave me an address and asked me to pass it along to you. Sixteen fifty-five North Cumberland, Miami, Florida."

Alonzo's hand tightened on the phone receiver. It was the address of one of his many drug warehouses. "Perhaps he knows a bit more than I thought."

"Another thing," Bender said. "You told me that Osborne didn't speak Spanish."

"He doesn't," Alonzo said.

"He does now," Bender said. "This afternoon he conducted our entire interview in fluent Spanish. He speaks it as well as you. He suggested that I let you know."

4

After Bender left, June drove us to the Federal Detention Center where they are keeping Dad. Agent Pelton met us at the front door and led us to a waiting room on the third floor. . . .

"Generally," Agent Pelton began, "we wouldn't allow you to speak to your husband prior to our interviewing you, Mrs. Osborne, but I think it might be in everyone's interest if we stretch the rules a little this time."

June nodded. "We appreciate you making this exception. I'm assuming there will be no recording devices."

"You assume correctly, Ms. Saunders. We consider this a privileged conversation between husband and wife." Agent Pelton pointed to the chairs along the wall. "You and the kids can wait here."

He led Patricia down a hallway to a metal door with a uniformed guard standing in front of it. He glanced at his watch. "You've got fifteen minutes, Mrs. Osborne." The guard opened the door and Patricia stepped inside.

Neil tried to get up when she entered but was hindered by the shackles that bound his ankles to the floor. "How are the kids?" he asked.

Patricia looked at him coldly. "Considering everything you've put them through, they're fine."

"I'm sorry about all of this, Pat. I . . ."

Patricia cut him off. "We don't have time for that right now, Neil. I only have fifteen minutes." She took a deep breath to steel herself against the waves of emotions washing over her. It took all of her strength and will to look at Neil without bursting into tears of rage. All that mattered to her was protecting the children.

"Has the DEA interviewed you yet?" Neil asked.

"No, but I promised Agent Pelton that he could if he allowed me to speak to you privately."

"Has Benjamin Bender contacted you?"

"Yes, but I have not retained him as my attorney."

"Don't—"

Patricia held her hand up. "You are in no position to tell me what to do."

"I was going to say, don't even speak to him again. If he calls on the phone hang up on him. If he comes to the door, don't open it."

This surprised her. She had expected Neil to try to talk her into getting rid of June and retaining Bender. "We're not at the house anymore, we're—"

"Don't tell me. It's better that I don't know." Neil looked down at his handcuffs. "Did they hurt you? Did they hurt the kids?"

"Not physically. But Joanne and Jack are traumatized.

Confused. It will be a long time before they forget the experience, if they ever do."

"And the police?"

"They took almost everything from the house, including the cars. I need to make some decisions, Neil. And you have to help me make them."

"Of course," he said quietly.

She took another deep breath. "Agent Pelton is going to ask about what happened last night. He knows something went on, but he doesn't know the specifics. One of the men last night said that he would kill you if we told anyone what happened to us. He said that he would kill us too."

"They'll try. How many were there?"

"Three. They wore ski masks."

"Probably Berry Jones and Paul Snider. Maybe even Alonzo Aznar. He likes getting his hands dirty from time to time."

"Who are they?"

"Alonzo Aznar runs a drug cartel. The two men with him are his right and left hands. But it would be best for you not to mention their names to Pelton. I'd rather do that myself when it comes down to it."

"The DEA took all your files and your computer."

"They won't find anything there."

"What should we do, Neil?"

He looked at her for a long time before answering. "You should tell Pelton what happened last night."

This was not the answer she was expecting. "Why?"

"Because I've already told him about it."

"I don't understand. They were very specific about what—"

"It was the only way to protect you and the kids," Neil said. "I told Pelton that I will tell him everything he wants to know as soon as I know that you're safe. He said he would put you and the kids into the Witness Security Program."

"What does that mean?"

Neil looked back down at table. "They'll auction everything off including the house and give you some of the proceeds after everything is settled. You'll probably be able to take a few things with you. Then they'll move you and the kids to a new town. Set you up in a small business if you want. You'll have new identities. You won't be able to contact our friends or family, but you and Jacko and Joanne will be safe. It means you'll have to start all over again, Pat, as if your real past never happened. It will be horrible, but it's better than the alternative. Alonzo and his people are vicious and they have long memories."

Patricia could not imagine what this would mean for her and Jack and Joanne. No contact with her past? Ever? "What about you?"

"I'm not important right now. The only thing that matters to me is you and the kids. We'll see about me later. How much time do we have?"

Patricia looked at her watch. "Less than five minutes."

"Okay. Here's what we'll do. I've got to keep up a good front, which means I have to keep Bender on as my attorney. He's Alonzo's man, as you've probably already guessed. When I talked to you last night I was with Bender. They called his cell phone. If I drop Bender, all bets are off.

Alonzo will know that I'm cooperating with the DEA and it's crucial that he doesn't get wind of this until after you're safe.

"I'll tell Bender that you wanted your own attorney—that I couldn't talk you out of it. I've already gotten word to Alonzo that nothing had better happen to you or the kids."

"What's going to stop him?"

"I told Bender that if anything happens to you, a certain document will make its way to the DEA and it will be all over for Alonzo and his operation. That should keep him at bay for a while."

"And is there such a document?"

"It doesn't matter if there is or isn't. If Alonzo thinks there is they won't do anything to you or me until they can figure out what to do about it. This will give Pelton a chance to get you out of town. We'll use June as a messenger. We can trust her. When she tells me that you're safe, I'll give Pelton the information he wants."

The door opened. "Time's up," the guard said.

"Are we clear on everything?" Neil asked.

Patricia nodded and stood up.

"I love you, Pat. I always will."

Patricia was so numbed by what had happened she could not respond.

"You have to leave now, Mrs. Osborne."

"One more thing," Neil said. "I want to see the kids before they put you in the program. It might be my last chance."

"I'll ask Agent Pelton," Patricia said. "I'll ask the kids."

Agent Pelton and June were waiting for her down the hallway.

"Are you ready to answer some questions for us, Mrs. Osborne?" Agent Pelton asked.

Patricia looked at June, who nodded. "I guess so."

The interview ended two hours later. After it was over, Agent Pelton led Patricia and June to the room where Jack and Joanne were waiting. Patricia stopped before opening the door. "Agent Pelton, I don't know how to put this," she said. "But I'm feeling kind of paranoid staying at the hotel. This whole thing has been so upsetting. . . ."

"You want protection," Agent Pelton said.

"I know it's silly."

Agent Pelton smiled for the first time since he had met them. "Mrs. Osborne, you've been under constant surveillance since the moment you left your house. We have three people at the hotel around the clock."

"But Benjamin Bender—"

"Famous attorneys are usually nonviolent." He glanced at June with a grin. "We didn't want to let him know we were keeping an eye on you, so we let him through."

"But how did he know where we were?"

Agent Pelton's smile disappeared. "You didn't call him?"

Patricia and June shook their heads.

5

When Mom came back into the waiting room I could tell she had been crying. I asked about Dad. She didn't answer me. Joanne asked about her interview with Agent Pelton. She said she would talk to us about it tomorrow.

I have a very bad feeling. It's hard to believe, but I think the worst is still to come. . . .

The phone next to Patricia Osborne's bed rang at 3 A.M. It was Agent Pelton.

"I think it's time for you to change hotels," he said.

Half awake, she looked out the window. "Can't we at least wait until it's light out? The kids are still asleep."

"No."

An inconspicuous van without passenger windows picked them up in back of the hotel.

"We sent a decoy family out a few minutes ago," Agent Pelton informed them. "Just in case."

This had been an unnecessary precaution. When the van

pulled away from the hotel, Berry Jones and Paul Snider were sound asleep in the front seat of their car.

After a short drive, the van turned off the road and came to a stop. When the Osbornes got out they were surprised to find themselves in their own garage. June Saunders was waiting for them. Standing next to her was a man and woman they had not met.

Agent Pelton introduced them. "This is Doris Welty and Donald Smites. They're United States Marshals."

Doris smiled. "We'll be spending a lot of time together during the next few weeks. We're handling all the details of your relocation. It might be awkward for you kids to call us Marshal Welty and Marshal Smites. So, why don't you just call us Uncle Don and Aunt Doris."

"Relocation?" Jack looked at his mother with confusion. "What's going on, Mom?"

"Your father has decided to cooperate with the Drug Enforcement Agency," she said. "He's going to tell them what he knows."

"After he has been assured that you're all safe," June added.

"What does that have to do with us?" Joanne asked.

"Let's go into the house," Agent Pelton suggested.

They sat down at the kitchen table.

"We're putting you into the Witness Security Program," Uncle Don explained. "That means we'll be providing you with new identities. You'll be moved to a new home, attend new schools—"

Joanne looked at her mother in shock. "You knew about this?"

"I knew it was a possibility," she answered. "But I didn't know it would happen so soon."

"It's much better if we move quickly," Uncle Don added. "We decided to take advantage of the hotel change by letting you tag all the things you want us to move."

"I don't understand," Joanne said.

"As soon as they figure out that you aren't at the hotel anymore they might stake out the house. We aren't going to give them that chance."

"Were we being watched at the hotel?" Jack asked.

"We don't know," Agent Pelton said. "But we're assuming you were. These people are professionals and have the best surveillance equipment that money can buy."

"After you've tagged your things we'll take you to a hotel out of town," Uncle Don continued.

"You'll be there until you're relocated," Doris said. "From this point on you can't contact anyone."

"What about our friends?" Joanne asked.

Aunt Doris shook her head. "I know this is hard, but it's the only way to keep you safe."

Hard? Jack thought. This is impossible. It's a nightmare. "For how long?"

"It's permanent," Uncle Don said.

Jack stared at him in stunned silence as this sunk in, then looked at his mother. "Why, Mom? We don't know anything. We didn't do anything wrong."

Agent Pelton answered for Mrs. Osborne. "I'm afraid that doesn't matter to these animals. They're after your father and the only way to get to him is through you."

"But if Dad tells you what you want to know, why

would they come after us?"

"To make a statement," Agent Pelton said. "To show their people what happens if they talk to us."

"What if you arrest them?" Joanne asked. "Do we get to come back here then?"

Agent Pelton shook his head. "I wish it were as simple as that. When your father tells us what he knows, the best we can do is stop some of the drugs they're sending across the border. We won't catch all the people running the ring. Most of them don't live in this country. They'll send people after you and your father. Men like the ones who broke into your house the other night. Maybe the same men. They'll pay them hundreds of thousands of dollars to hurt you."

Aunt Doris put her hand on Joanne's shoulders. "We can't keep you under protective custody forever, but we can hide you so securely that they will never be able to find you."

"This can't be happening." Joanne began to cry. "How could Dad do this to us?"

Patricia put her arms around her.

Uncle Don stood up. "We don't have a lot of time. We need to have you out of here before daybreak." He reached into his pocket and came out with a bunch of red tags. "We have moving boxes upstairs. You'll need to pack your things and tag whatever you want to take. But I'm warning you— I don't know where you'll be moving to, but I can guarantee you it won't be as big as this place. You can't take it all with you."

It didn't take Jack long to fill up three moving boxes with the things he wanted from his bedroom. He looked around at what was left and decided he didn't need another box. There was just one more item to pack. He slipped down the stairs and out the back door without anyone seeing him. He crossed the backyard, finding it difficult to believe that this was the last time he would ever go into his father's workshop.

When he had completed his first journal, Jack had brought it to his father and asked where he should keep it.

"That's the problem with diaries," his father had mused. "How do you keep your private thoughts private after you write them down? I think we should build a special journal box. We'll put a lock on it and find the perfect place to stash it."

They had spent the rest of the day and part of the next working on the box. It was made of varnished hardwood, deep enough to hold several journals. Jack's father put a clasp on the lid so the box could be locked, and as a final touch, he attached a brass plate to the box engraved with the words *Jack in the Box*.

"Very funny, Dad."

"I thought so, too. Here's the key." His father gave him a chain with a key suspended on it. "I'll keep a backup key in case you lose yours."

Jack put the key around his neck.

"And I have the perfect place to hide the box," his father told him, squatting down on the floor in front of his workbench. "If you undo these two screws, this front panel comes off." He handed Jack a screwdriver.

Jack twisted the screws out. Underneath the panel was a small shelf. He slipped the box in and replaced the panel.

"There you go." His father smiled at him.

But Jack was still not convinced. "You know the secret place and you have a key to the box."

His father put his right hand over his heart and said, "Jacko, I promise I will never read your diaries. Good enough?"

"Good enough."

And as far as Jack knew, his father had not broken that promise in the five years he had been using the Jack in the Box. When he turned the shop light on, he was relieved to see the panel was still in place and that the DEA had not found it. He unscrewed the panel. The box was exactly where he had left it eight months earlier when he had put his last journal in it.

Back inside the house everyone was so busy packing they didn't even glance at the small wooden box he had under his arm. He took it up to his bedroom and put it into a cardboard moving box underneath Commander IF's space shuttle.

After everything was packed, the Osbornes gathered in the empty kitchen with June Saunders. They stood for a long time without a saying a word in the place they had once considered the heart of their home.

"I guess this is it," June sighed. "After this, we won't be able to have any more direct contact. If you need me you'll have to go through the U.S. Marshals."

"Why?" Patricia asked. "You're my attorney."

"In case I'm being watched. They don't want me leading them to you."

"But Neil said you're the only one he trusts to tell him that we're safe."

"I've thought about that. When you think you're safe, just send me a simple postcard with nothing written on it."

"I've got just the thing," Jack said excitedly, and ran back up to the box in his room. He came back to the kitchen holding a blank postcard he had gotten when they visited the Kennedy Space Center. On it was a photo of a space shuttle coming in for a landing.

"That will do," June nodded. "When you think everything's okay, send it to me. As soon as I get it, I'll go see Neil and tell him he can proceed."

Patricia put the postcard into her purse.

"They're gone," Berry said into the phone.

There was a very long silence on the other end of the line followed by a simple question from Alonzo Aznar. "When?"

"We're not exactly sure," Berry said. "They must have slipped out in the middle of the night. Paul and me couldn't cover all the exits by ourselves."

"You have checked the house?"

"Yeah. They're not there and by the looks of things they're not going back. Not much left inside."

"I'll be in touch."

Alonzo's next call was to Benjamin Bender. When that unpleasant conversation was over, Bender took a taxi to the Federal Detention Center to speak with his client, Neil Osborne.

"Our friend was quite surprised when he learned you spoke Spanish."

43

Neil grinned. "I bet he was."

"On a totally different subject," Bender added, "it seems that your family unexpectedly checked out of their hotel."

"Checked out?" Neil tried to act surprised.

"Our concern," Bender continued, "is *why* they left the hotel. Your wife comes by to see you last night and a few hours later they leave."

"It's news to me." Pelton had told him that morning they had moved them. Neil hoped Alonzo didn't know where they were.

"What did you discuss during your visit?" Bender asked.

"I spent the whole time trying to talk her into dumping June Saunders and letting you handle things, but she wouldn't go for it. She doesn't trust you."

"Do you?"

"There's no one else I can trust."

"That's correct." Bender nodded in approval. "She hasn't told anyone about her visitors?"

"She's knows what will happen if she talks. What are you getting at?"

"We're wondering if you've made a deal with the DEA in exchange for protecting your family."

"Not yet," Neil said. "But I will if you lay a finger on my family again."

"We won't as long as you do exactly what we say."

"Then we don't have a problem."

Bender stared at Neil for a very long time. Neil met his gaze, but couldn't tell if Bender was buying his story or not.

Thursday, August 17

We are being kept like prisoners in our new hotel. They have taken the phones away. "To remove the temptation," Aunt Doris told us. Uncle Don was a lot more blunt: "You don't know anybody and nobody knows you. What good is a phone?"

When the housekeeper comes to clean, we're shuffled into the adjoining room until she's finished. We never go outside, and the tans we got over the summer have faded to the color of egg salad.

Things are weird, which Aunt Doris says is perfectly normal under the circumstances. I think the reason they have kept us here this long is so we'll be eager to start our new life. If I have to endure another day of "indoctrination" (as Uncle Don calls it) I might lose my mind. Day after day, and hour after hour we discuss our cover story, who to watch out for, and how to handle it if one of us slips up.

A psychologist came by one day and interviewed us individually.

and in a group. Somehow she got me talking about my caped-crusader days and seemed particularly interested in my wearing Joanne's red leotards. After this I decided to skip mentioning Commander IF, fearing Marshal Shrink would put me in a straightjacket.

But the thing that's really bugging me is that Mom and Joanne never mention Dad anymore. It's like he never existed or something. . . .

Jack refused to dye his hair blond.

"But we have to change your appearance," Aunt Doris said. "It's for your own safety."

"No," Jack insisted. "If you bleach my hair I'll look like an albino. What kind of disguise is that?"

Aunt Doris shook her head. "You're really missing the spirit of all this."

"Heather's coming by today to give you a hand," Uncle Don said.

"Heather?"

Jack's question was answered by a knock on the door. Heather was some kind of federal beautician. She came into the room pushing a trunk on wheels. "It's makeover time!" She gave them an enthusiastic smile, opened her trunk, and pulled out a pile of fashion magazines. "Your dreams are about to come true!"

The answer to Jack's dream was not in the trunk, unless Heather had the key to his father's cell hidden there. His mother and sister were hesitant at first, but Heather won them over. Within minutes the three of them were pointing at photographs and giggling as if they were at a slumber party.

A vote was taken. "The Grangers will be blue-eyed blonds!" Heather announced.

Not this Granger, Jack thought, refusing to participate in the vote. He liked his brown hair and brown eyes. He sat in the corner and watched uncomfortably as Heather snipped, combed, teased, and dyed his mother and sister. When Heather finished, they looked like twins. He would not have recognized them if he hadn't seen the transformation himself.

"And now for the final touch!" Heather took out a small case filled with colored contact lenses (none of the Osbornes wore glasses). With lenses in place, the Granger twins had matching blue eyes.

"You're next, Jack."

He shook his head. "You're not dying my hair blond."

Heather looked like he had slapped her in the face, but recovered quickly with a bright smile. "The girls will go crazy over you!"

"No."

His mother ordered him into the adjoining room. "Jack, you've got to go along with this."

"No I don't."

"Please."

"What am I going to do when my real hair starts to grow in?" His hair was dark brown, like his father's.

"You'll dye it like we do. It only takes a few minutes. There's nothing to it. Women do this all the time. "

"I'm not a woman. What about gym class?"

She stared at him, not understanding.

Jack turned red with embarrassment. It finally dawned

on her what he was talking about. "Oh," she said. "I see what you mean."

They walked back into the other room. Heather cut Jack's hair, but she didn't dye it. Any of it. She taught him how to put in the blue contacts, which was not easy. Jack wasn't used to having foreign objects anywhere near his eyes and blinked every time the contact came in for a landing, but Heather finally prevailed. He was now a blue-eyed boy.

A week later Uncle Don told them that everything was in place for their relocation. They were leaving in the morning. "From now on, you are the Grangers. I want you to use your new names even when you are talking privately to each other."

"And," Aunt Doris added, "we've arranged to have you see your dad before you go."

"I don't want to see him," Wanda said.

Aunt Doris looked confused. "But it might be your last chance for a very long time."

"I still don't want to." Wanda said angrily and stamped into the adjoining room and slammed the door.

"I do," Zach said. It was all he had been thinking about for the past three weeks.

Two hours later, Zach and his mother were put into a van and driven to the Federal Detention Center. Agent Pelton led them down a hallway to a door with a uniformed guard standing in front of it. The guard opened the door and told them to go in. When they got inside Zach's mother stayed near the door. "I'll stand here," she said.

Zach stared at his father with alarm. He was pale and had lost a lot of weight. He wore a bright orange short-sleeved jumpsuit. Silver manacles were locked around his wrists and ankles. He was seated at a metal table with a green enamel top. His leg manacles ran through an eyebolt screwed into the floor so he couldn't get off the stool he was sitting on. The room had one window. The glass was frosted so you couldn't see out, and the frame was covered with heavy wire mesh so you couldn't get out.

"I'm sorry you had to see me this way, Jacko," his father said.

Zach sat on the stool opposite his father and stared down at the table. The green enamel surface was carved with graffiti.

"How have you been?" his father asked.

Zach could not seem to raise his head.

"I'm so sorry about all this." His father's voice was choked with emotion.

Zach felt hot tears on his cheeks.

"Is Joanne here?" Neil Osborne asked, glancing at Mary. She stared at her feet. She didn't answer.

"No," Zach managed to say. Tears splattered on the tabletop.

"I wanted a chance to explain things to you myself." His father swallowed hard. "I'm not sure when we'll be seeing each other again."

Zach looked up from the table. "But you'll come to live with us when you get this all straightened out."

"I don't know," his father spoke in almost in a whisper. "It's better this way, for now. Safer." He looked down at his

49

hands for a moment. "This whole thing's my fault, Jacko. Joanne and you and your mom have every right to be disgusted with me."

"I'm not disgusted." Zach wasn't sure how he felt at the moment. Confused. Sad. Scared. Perhaps all three at once. "When are they going to let you out?"

"I don't know, son. It could be a long time."

"But if you tell the DEA what they want to know. . . ."

"We haven't gotten that far, Jacko. The problem is that they already know a lot. So, I have to tell them things they don't know. Things that will help them. I'm not sure that I know enough to get out of here."

The idea of his father staying in jail had never occurred to Zach. He felt sick to his stomach.

"I want to tell you what happened," his father said. "I wanted to tell Joanne too. I guess it will be up to you to tell her when she decides she wants to hear it."

Zach did not think this would be anytime in the near future.

"I ran into money problems soon after I bought the airline company," his father began. "I had to mortgage everything we owned to keep it going. I couldn't make my loan payments and the bank was going to take everything. I was desperate. I didn't know what to do. Then I met a man in Colombia named Alonzo Aznar. He offered to bail me out. I sold him part of the company and in return, he paid off my debts."

His father took a deep breath. "What I'm going to tell you next is very hard for me. But I promised myself that if I got a chance I would tell you the truth regardless of what you might think of me. I'm not going to candy-coat this, Jacko. Alonzo Aznar runs a drug cartel. The men who came to the house and threatened you are his men."

Zach did not want to ask his next question because he was afraid of the answer. "Did you know about the cartel before you started working for it?"

His father looked directly at him. "I'm not going to lie to you, Jacko. I'm ashamed to admit it, but I knew what his business was and what I would be doing for him. I told myself that I'd do it for a year, get the company back on its feet, then break off the partnership."

He continued looking at Zach without wavering.

"There's something else. I liked what I was doing, Jacko. The money was fabulous and I liked Alonzo. We became friends. I guess I went a little crazy. The year came and went. I had more money than I knew what to do with, but then I didn't want to leave."

"What about all the drugs you were bringing into the country?"

"That was part of the craziness, and with the exception of what I did to you, the part I regret the most. I didn't think about the harm I was causing. I told myself that if I didn't fly for them, someone else would. My thinking was totally screwed up—totally wrong.

"Your mom and I started to have problems. I don't want to go into details, but I want you to know that the problems were caused entirely by me. I also want you to know that she didn't have the slightest idea what I was doing. As far as she knew I was flying legitimate cargo. You've got to believe me on this."

Zach did. He glanced at his mother. She was still standing next to the door with her head down. She hated drugs of any kind. She didn't smoke. She didn't drink alcohol. She was even reluctant to take over-the-counter remedies for headaches and other aches and pains.

His father held his manacled wrists up. "It's easy to have regrets after you've been caught. But I deserve to be wearing these things. I deserve to be in prison. What I did was wrong. I gave up everything I loved and nearly got you all killed. I can't undo what I've done, but as soon as you're safe I'm going to do everything in my power to break up this cartel. I am going to tell them what I know so I can live with myself. I'm going to tell them because it's the right thing to do."

Zach's mother let out an anguished sob and fled through the door.

The guard stepped inside. Zach's father waved him away, but the guard stayed where he was. "Do you still have the Jack in the Box?"

Zach nodded.

"Good. Keep it safe. Do you take off tomorrow?"

"Yes."

"I wish I was going with you."

"I do, too."

"I'm afraid you're going to have to leave, son," the guard said.

Zach stood and walked around the table to his father. He put his arms around him. "I love you, Dad."

"That means more to me than you'll ever know, Jacko."

* * *

At Salt Lake City the Grangers were the last to get off the airplane. A black van was waiting for them on the tarmac beneath the jet way. In the front seat were two bulky men wearing suits. The Grangers climbed in the back and Uncle Don slid the door closed. "Everything set?"

"We're clear," the driver said and stepped on the accelerator.

So it's Salt Lake City, Zach thought. But it wasn't. They drove for about fifteen minutes and pulled into the parking lot of a large shopping mall.

"Here's your new car." Aunt Doris pointed to a metallic gray minivan and held a set of keys out to Mrs. Granger. The minivan was old. The driver's door had a big dent in it.

"Nice wheels," Zach commented. His mother gave him a tired look and took the keys. They had left behind a Range Rover and a red Mercedes convertible. When Mrs. Granger was Mrs. Osborne she would not have dreamed of driving a minivan. Now she owned one. Zach looked at his sister for her reaction. There was none. Wanda was not wavering from the *I must be courageous* role she had adopted almost from the moment this awful thing had happened to them.

Zach helped Uncle Don transfer their bags into the back of the minivan and saw that the license plate was from Nevada. "So we're moving to Nevada."

"Smart kid." Uncle Don pointed at a green Ford Taurus parked across from the minivan. "Doris will ride with you and I'll lead in our rental." He looked at Wanda. "Anyone want to ride with me?" Wanda smiled, but didn't say yes.

The man who had driven them from the airport scanned

the parking lot. "Looks clean. You want us to tail you a ways just in case?"

Uncle Don shook his head. "I think we're in good shape, here."

The black van drove away.

Wanda finally spoke up. "I'll ride with Uncle Don."

Zach got into the backseat of the minivan behind his mother and Aunt Doris, and they followed the Ford Taurus.

"Las Vegas or Reno?" Zach asked.

His mother looked at Aunt Doris.

"Lake Tahoe?" Zach couldn't think of any other cities in Nevada.

"It's safe to tell him now," Aunt Doris said.

His mother looked at Zach in the rearview mirror. "Elko."

"Where?"

"Elko, Nevada."

"Where's that?"

"Three and a half hours from here."

"Up in the mountains," Aunt Doris added. "It's beautiful. You'll like it."

No I won't, Zach thought.

And he was right.

To Zach the word *mountains* meant the Rockies, the Cascades, the Himalayas. The Nevada mountains were short, brown, ragged rocks. The town of Elko lay at the base of the rocks. Commander IF said the landscape looked like Mars.

"It's a desert."

"I love the desert," his mother said.

"Then why didn't you pick Palm Springs?"

"It wasn't on the list," Mrs. Granger explained. "And even if it had been, Jack—sorry . . . Zach—we couldn't afford to live there. Please don't make this any more difficult than it already is."

Zach wished the Ford Taurus was behind them so he could turn around and see his sister's face. He bet Commander IF a million dollars that her mouth was hanging open in utter horror. Commander IF did not take the bet.

They turned off the freeway onto a busy street and drove past hotels, gambling casinos with flashing lights, the Northeastern Nevada Museum, and a small shopping mall, which Aunt Doris pointed to and said, "That's where your space is."

"Where?" Mrs. Granger craned her neck.

"Between the coffee shop and the grocery store."

"What space?" Zach asked.

"I think it's a good spot," Aunt Doris continued. "Idaho Street is the main road through town. There's a lot of local traffic and there's a big casino right across the street with busloads of gamblers."

"What space?" Zach asked a little louder.

"I'm opening a bookstore," his mother explained, which was news to Zach. In their previous life his mother had been a very successful realtor.

"Why?" Zach asked.

"I worked in a bookstore all through college and I loved it. I'm tired of selling houses, but I've got to make a living. I can't work in the gold mine and I'm not going to become a cocktail waitress or a card dealer at one of the casinos."

Zach's father had gotten tired of his job, too, and that was the reason they had become the Grangers. "What gold mine?" he asked.

"One of the biggest in the United States," Aunt Doris said. "Most people in Elko work for the mine in one way or another."

"Will we get free books?" Zach asked.

"A lot of free books."

Zach was happy to hear this. They continued down Idaho Street, passing through downtown Elko, which had more pickup trucks parked along the curb than cars and more cowboy boots on people's feet than shoes. Yippee-ki-yay! Commander IF said. Turning off Idaho they entered a neighborhood of small houses with trees growing in front of them, which Zach was glad to see.

"I was beginning to think that nothing grew here higher than our knees," Zach commented.

No one laughed.

The streets all had tree names like Pine, Juniper, Oak, Cedar, Fir, Ash, and Maple. They took a right on Elm Street and pulled over to the curb.

"Mrs. Granger, here's your new house," Aunt Doris announced.

Zach's mother shut the engine off. "Oh." Her disappointment was obvious.

"I know it's not exactly what you're used to," Aunt Doris said quickly. "But it's the best we could do right now. Gold prices are up and it's difficult to find affordable rentals. And as you know, we didn't have much time to relocate you."

Zach's parents had never rented a house in their lives. The house they had left behind had had 5,000 square feet. This house looked smaller than their former garage.

"You said there were three bedrooms," Mrs. Granger said.

"There are, but they're small."

Zach opened the van's sliding door. Ignoring the blast of dry heat, he hurried over to the Taurus, not wanting to miss a second of his sister's shock. He wasn't disappointed. Her mouth hung open and her blue eyes, which used to be brown, looked like they were going to pop out of their sockets. This was nothing compared to her reaction when she saw her bedroom, which was smaller than her closet at their old house. She began to cry, but the house was so hot that her mascara-tinted tears evaporated before they got halfway down her checks.

Zach's bedroom was even smaller, but it didn't bother him much. Less space to clean. Commander IF liked the room too—it was just his size.

Uncle Don banged his shin on a cardboard box that had fallen from one of the many precarious stacks moved to the tiny house the week before. "It seemed a lot bigger when it was empty."

"What will we do with everything?" Mrs. Granger asked.

"I warned you that you couldn't take it all with you," Uncle Don said.

Zach's mother and Aunt Doris shot him a look. "We didn't take it all with us," Mrs. Granger said icily. "*You* took most of what we owned."

Uncle Don started to protest, but Aunt Doris cut him off.

"Don, why don't you go out and see if you can find us some food?" She pushed him toward the front door, which was about five steps from the kitchen.

"Want to come with me, Zach?" Uncle Don asked.

Zach shook his head, and Uncle Don left, happy to get out of there.

Mrs. Granger stared hopelessly at the strewn furniture and stacks of boxes. "What are we going to do, Doris?"

Aunt Doris put her arm around Mrs. Granger's shoulders. "We'll unpack what we can and rent a storage unit for the rest. A bigger place is bound to come up. Consider this your temporary home until then."

Part Two

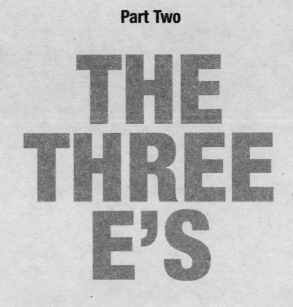

THE THREE E'S

Tuesday, August 29

My room is more like an enclosed hallway than a bedroom. I can stand in the middle of it with my arms spread and touch two of the walls with my fingertips.

Aunt Doris and Uncle Don have been helping us unpack and move the stuff the house can't hold to a storage place. Midway through the first day we found two air-conditioning units, which was a huge relief. The units sound like chain saws, but we don't care. During the day, the house is like the inside of an active volcano.

Last night we went over to Mom's space, which is exactly what it is—a big empty space that seems even more empty after our temporary "shack," as Mom calls it.

They started talking about where the bookshelves, counter, and cash register would go. ~~Joanne~~ Wanda began measuring the space with a steel tape measure. I sat down on the floor and watched. Mom said that she wanted to open the store by November so she can take advantage of the Christmas buying season.

While they were talking, Uncle Don came over to me and asked if I wanted to go for a walk. I told him that I didn't feel like it. He made it clear that it wasn't a request, which meant we were going for a talk, not a walk. This is not the first time we've had one of those.

Uncle Don is probably in his early thirties. Brown hair, brown eyes, over six feet tall, and in great shape. He resembles Dad in a lot of ways, but he doesn't have Dad's sense of humor.

We crossed Idaho Street, which wasn't very busy at that time of night, and walked past the casino parking lot, that was full of buses, cars, and RVs. It was cool out and I wished I'd brought my jacket. When the sun sets over Elko it's like switching a heater off.

Uncle Don told me I would have to keep my eyes open. That if I saw anyone hanging around our house or school who didn't look or feel right I was supposed to have Mom call him immediately.

"If there's a problem," he said, "we can be in Elko in a matter of hours."

I asked him if anyone in Elko knew who we really were. He said nobody knew—not the police, not the school I was going to, no one. As far as anyone in Elko knows, we are the Grangers from Portland, Oregon. Our father took off a couple years ago and Mom moved Wanda and me down here because she was tired of the city . . . blah, blah, blah . . . "If you slip up and blow your cover," he told me, "no matter how minor it might seem, I want you to tell your mother."

This made me mad. Everyone thinks I'm the one who is going

to slip up. *He said that from his experience people my age have a hard time grasping the fact that we and our families are in real danger. He couldn't remember how many times they've had to relocate a family because "a kid" told a friend, girlfriend, or boyfriend who they really were.*

Uncle Don and Aunt Doris took off a couple hours ago, saying they hoped they never saw us again, which would mean that our relocation was a success. I knew they would have to leave one day, but I didn't think it would be so soon. One or both of them have been with us for the past month. Aunt Doris said it was time for the Granger family to get on with their lives.

If you take the "v" out of lives, what do you get?

Mom has the space shuttle postcard pinned to the refrigerator with a magnet. Every time I see it I think of Dad. I wonder how long it will be before she sends it?

"You've got to get a grip, Zach," Wanda said.

Zach closed his journal. He was sitting on the sofa in the living/dining/family room watching a black-and-white John Wayne World War II movie on television as he wrote. The screen was so close to the sofa it was like watching the movie in a theater.

Their mother had gone to the bookstore to interview contractors. Zach had wondered why his sister had not gone with her like she usually did. Now he knew. Wanda had stayed home to have a heart-to-heart with her little brother.

"Zach?"

He resented how easily this name came out of her mouth, as if he had been born with it.

"Are you listening to me?" She would have blocked his

view if there had been room in front of the television and his face.

"It's sort of hard not to," Zach sighed.

"All you've done since we moved in here is to sit around and watch these stupid movies and mess up the house. Your legs aren't broken anymore. What's your excuse now?"

Zach ignored the question. "These old movies are great. You could learn something from these actors."

She glanced at the tube. "I don't think John Wayne has much to teach me, unless we go to war with Japan again."

"You never know."

"You're scaring me, Zach. And what's more, you're worrying Mom and she has enough to think about without—"

"Oh, please." Zach dismissed her.

"I'm serious!" Wanda raised her voice. "Are you going to spend the rest of your life watching television and writing in that stupid journal of yours? Aren't you even a little curious about Elko?"

She waited for him to defend himself. Zach didn't—knowing that it would bug her a lot more than anything he could say.

"I know what you're trying to do, Zach," she said. "And it's not going to work."

Jack and Joanne had gotten along pretty well until Joanne became a sophomore in high school. Up until then they had been able to talk about any and everything. Jack had even told her about Commander IF, and she hadn't laughed or made fun of him. But things had changed between them. For instance, Zach wouldn't think of telling her that Commander IF had returned from Mars. Nor was he going to discuss why he was sitting in front of the television all day long, something he had never done in the past. Zach didn't understand it himself.

He had heard someplace that a tragedy usually brings a family closer together. He was learning that this was only partially true. Their tragedy had certainly brought his mother and sister closer together, but somehow the whirlwind had failed to snap Zach up along with them.

"You're impossible, Zach!" Wanda shouted and stomped three steps away into her bedroom and slammed the door.

Zach believed it was the theater that had separated him and his sister. The summer after her freshman year she had joined a local theater group and found her calling in life. "I'm going to be an actress," she announced rather dramatically at dinner one night.

That summer he saw her perform in three musicals. He had to admit that she was pretty good. She started hanging around with a group called The Thespians at her high school. His parents got her acting, singing, and dance lessons. And somehow she was transformed into a beautiful being with perfect hair, body, nails, and makeup. She began talking funny and staying in her roles around the house. Zach's friends hung around the house gawking at her lustfully, which Zach found slightly nauseating. Wanda didn't look like his sister, sound like his sister, or act like his sister. And now she didn't even have his sister's name.

Zach switched the television off and stashed his journal in his laundry hamper underneath his underwear, figuring anyone willing to dig for it there deserved to read it. He walked out onto the front porch and watched a lizard scurry up the siding. "That's a dragon to you, Commander IF," he said. Then he yelled back inside that he was going for a walk.

Zach wandered down the sidewalk wondering how his sister would feel if she knew she would be stuck in Elko for the next five years like he was going to be. After her senior year, the plan was for Wanda to go to college at UCLA in Los Angeles, not far from Hollywood.

Maybe the famous Wanda Granger will let me spend the summers at her mansion cleaning the pool and mowing her huge lawn, Zach fantasized. If her career started to wane she could write an autobiography confessing that her real name was Joanne Osborne. This would get her on all of the talk shows, which would lead to a remarkable comeback career.

About five blocks from their house Zach came to a school that looked about a hundred years old. The building was a gigantic brick structure three stories tall. The sign outside read:

ELKO MIDDLE SCHOOL
CLASSES BEGIN SEPTEMBER 5TH
HOPE YOU HAD A SUPER SUMMER!

"Super *weird* is more like it," Zach muttered, wondering if this was his new school. He walked up the stairs to the front door with the intention of just peeking through the window and found the door unlocked. He stepped inside and was surprised to hear piano music echoing throughout the building. He looked in the office, hoping to ask someone if the school went up to seventh grade, but no one was there.

He followed the music down a wide hallway lined with open, institutional-green lockers that smelled as if they had just been sprayed with disinfectant. The music led him to a dim auditorium, which was unlike any grade-school auditorium he had ever seen. It was huge, with row after row of velvet-covered chairs facing a wide stage with an orchestra pit in front of it. On either side of the stage were elevated box seats. Below the boxes hung lush velvet curtains, which were the same shade of blue as the chairs and stage curtains. Above him was a full balcony. The music came from a grand piano on the stage. The only light on the stage came from a small lamp lighting the sheet music and keyboard. Zach could not see the man playing, but he could hear his deep tenor voice. The words were overwhelmed by the powerful music, and so was Zach. It filled his chest and made his legs weak. He sank into the nearest seat and listened.

After the piece ended, the last chord echoed through the auditorium as if it did not want to leave. Zach felt like applauding, but held his hands in his lap quietly because he wasn't sure he was supposed to be there. The sheet music rustled as the pianist removed it from the holder. The piano bench scraped against the wooden floor. The man stepped into the dim light at the edge of the stage and looked out into the dark auditorium. Zach was surprised at the man's appearance. He had expected a refined gentleman with long delicate fingers, and white swept-back hair. A tuxedo with tails would not have shocked him. But the man standing on the edge of the stage was nothing like that. He was dressed in work clothes: khaki pants, matching shirt, and heavy boots. Hanging on his belt was a ring with at least fifty keys dangling from it. He wore a pair of dark-framed glasses. What was left of his hair was very short and gray. Zach guessed the man was in his mid-sixties, and for his age he seemed to be in unusually good shape. His shirtsleeves were rolled up to his biceps, which bulged under the pressure. His powerful arms hung from a thick, muscular torso mounted on a narrow waist. If Zach had not seen the man get up from the piano, he would not have believed that this was the same man who had just played and sung the beautiful song.

"Well, what did you think of it?" the man asked.

Zach slumped in his seat. It squeaked loudly.

"Stay in that seat!" the man shouted. "I mean it. Don't move! I've been looking for that squeak since last spring." He hurried offstage and before Zach could decide whether he should leave or stay, the house lights came on and, a moment later, the man walked through a small door near the stage carrying a toolbox.

"You can get up now," the man said. When Zach stood, the seat groaned. "What are the chances? I swear I've sat in every seat in the house a dozen times—including the one you're sitting in—looking for that abomination and this is the first time I've heard it sound off outside of a performance. I'm grateful to you—?"

"Jack." It was out of his mouth before he knew what he was saying. Commander IF winced.

"Jack what?"

"It's *Zach*. Zach Granger."

"Well, my name's Sam Sebesta, but most people around

here call me Sam." He held out a rough, callused hand that did not look like it could play a grand piano. Zach shook it, hoping that he had pulled off the name change smoothly. "You're new at this school," Sam said.

"I'm not sure this is my school."

"Where do you live?"

"Over on Elm. I'll be in seventh grade."

"This is your school then. We go up to eighth grade here."

"Well, thanks." Zach turned to leave.

"Hold on a second. What's your hurry?"

"I just came in to find out if this is my school."

"Are you new to town or just to the neighborhood?"

"We're from Portland, Oregon," Zach said.

Sam's glasses hung from a string around his neck. He stared at Zach with the most startling blue eyes Zach had ever seen.

"My mom's opening a bookstore in town," Zach adding, hoping it sounded more convincing.

Sam continued to stare.

Zach looked away. "I've never seen a grade school with a theater this nice," he said, desperate to change the subject.

"This used to be the high school before they built the new one," Sam told him. "They were going to tear this theater down, but we convinced them to refurbish the theater instead. Saved them a lot of money, because they didn't have to build a regular auditorium at the high school."

"The high school uses this theater?"

"For their big performances, anyway. And sometimes

entertainers swing through town on their way to Las Vegas or Reno for one-night stands here."

Zach wanted to leave before the subject got back to where he was from. "I better be going."

"I'll walk out with you."

Sam put his toolbox on the seat to mark it and walked Zach to the front door of the school. "I guess I'll see you next Tuesday, Zach. Welcome to Elko."

"Thanks." Zach started through the door, then stopped. "I liked the song you were playing."

Sam grinned. "It's one of the pieces for this year's High School musical we're doing based on *The Phantom of the Opera*."

Zach had seen *The Phantom of the Opera* twice with his parents and sister. Wanda had played the CD for weeks and Zach knew every song. "I saw the musical in New York with my parents," Zach said. "I don't recognize that song."

"With good reason," Sam said. "We're doing our own version here. All new music. We're calling it *The Opera Ghost* and we're putting a lot more of the novel into the production."

"The ghost's name is Eric," Zach said.

Sam's blue eyes widened. "You've read the novel?"

Zach nodded. "Written by Gaston Leroux in nineteen ten." It was one of the books he had read in the hospital.

"Well, that's going to please your teachers. I bet there isn't a student in the whole school who's read the original novel. In fact, I doubt many of the teachers have read it either."

"I like adventure stories."

"That's something we have in common, then."

"What do you do here at the school?" Zach thought he must be the music instructor or theater director.

"I'm the custodian," Sam said.

Wednesday, August 30

I got into a little trouble last night. . . .

After meeting Sam (who is the strangest custodian I've ever met) I continued my walk, thinking I'd drop by Mom's bookstore to see how it was going.

I didn't get that far. On the way, I passed the Northeast Nevada Museum and went in for a quick look around. I should have known better. When I get into a museum I can't seem to leave until I've seen every exhibit and read every sign in the building. This used to drive my parents and sister crazy. It got to the point where they wouldn't take me to museums anymore.

I learned that the Ruby Mountains were not given their name because there were rubies there. The early settlers found garnets in the mountains and mistook them for rubies. Pretty disappointing.

I found out that herds of mastodons once roamed the plains below the Ruby Mountains. The museum has the bones and tusks to prove it.

Elko was built in 1868 about the same time they were laying tracks through Nevada for the transcontinental railway. There are 18,420 people here. 18,423 now, not counting Commander IF.

I wandered into a new wing they had just opened. It was filled with dead animals—moose, mountain goats, mountain sheep, mountain lions, deer, antelope, elk, bears, and several African animals, including half of a giraffe whose hindquarters disappeared into a wall.

The exhibit I spent the most time looking at was called: "Amerikanauk! Basques in the High Desert." I had never heard of the Basque people before. Apparently there are a lot of them here. They came over from Spain and France to herd sheep, which seemed like an awfully long way to travel for that kind of job. Sheep herding is not as common as it once was, but there are still a few Basques up in the hills who make their living this way. I was only about three quarters through the exhibit when a woman who worked for the museum told me they were closing. When I got outside I was surprised to see that it was getting dark. There wasn't time to visit Mom's store, so I headed home.

As soon as I got inside Mom and ~~Joanne~~ Wanda started yelling at me. Where had I been? What was I doing? Blah, blah, blah . . . They were totally panicked. At first I thought that the bad guys had found out where we were, but this wasn't it at all. Mom said she had called the police and they were out looking for me.

All because I was a little late getting home? I couldn't believe it. I told them where I had been and when they heard the word "museum" that seemed to calm them down some knowing what happens to me when I get inside one.

While I was explaining, there was a knock on the door and Wanda let in a young Elko cop named Officer Pinckney. He said *he had just dropped by to say they hadn't spotted me yet. Mom introduced me. So much for the efficiency of the Elko police department. It wasn't like I had tried to hide from them. I had strolled home down the busiest street in town.*

Anyway, he said that he would call the "search" off. Some search. Mom showed him to the front door, as if he couldn't find it himself—although you never know, he didn't find me. As soon as he was gone Mom went to bed saying that she was exhausted. She promised to continue our conversation this morning, meaning I'm going to get another lecture. At this rate I'll have heard enough lectures to earn a college diploma before I get out of grade school.

Zach's mother waited until after he had eaten breakfast before calling him into the living/dining/family room for the lecture.

"What do you have to say for yourself?"

"Nothing," Zach answered. "I didn't do anything wrong. If I stay in the house Wanda gets mad at me. If I leave, you get mad at me. I can't win."

"You don't seem to understand the situation we're in, Zach." She sat down next to him. "You have to tell me where you are going and when you'll be back. Wanda is handling our situation beautifully, but you seem to be having a problem."

Zach was pretty sick of hearing this. "I might be handling it in the same way if I knew that next year at this time I would be in Los Angeles trying to become a movie star. But no, Mom, Zach Granger will be right here in Elko, Nevada, probably still getting in trouble for doing horrible things like visiting museums!"

His mother smiled reluctantly. "I guess I might have overreacted a bit."

This was the first time Zach had seen her smile in a long time. He grinned. "A bit?"

"Well, maybe more than a bit." She put her arm around his shoulders and gave him a hug. "I guess I still haven't gotten over that terrible night."

None of them had.

Alonzo was sitting in one of the comfortable seats on his jet, which had just landed at the airport. Sitting across from him was a man known as El Sereno, The Watchman.

"We are concentrating our efforts on June Saunders," El Sereno reported. "Patricia Osborne and she are lifelong friends. We have bugged her home and office, tapped her cell phone, and we have a copy of her post-office-box key. We have even accessed her E-mail account."

"What about Agent Pelton and the other DEA people?"

"We are watching them as well, but I'm confident that June Saunders is the one who will lead us to the Osbornes."

"Has Ms. Saunders been to see Neil?"

"No."

"Has anyone been to see Neil?"

"Bender, Pelton, and some other DEA agents," El Sereno said. "We have someone on the inside of the detention center checking the visitation logs."

"Can your contact get to Neil?"

"No. They keep him totally isolated. The DEA is not even allowing him to leave his cell for exercise, and they are personally bringing him his food so we cannot poison him."

Alonzo stood up. "This has been very disruptive to business. We need to find out what Neil has on us, then eliminate him."

Alonzo walked down the aisle to the cockpit and said something to the pilot, then returned. "Every day this continues we are in greater danger. You must find out where the family is."

The jet engines started.

El Sereno stood up. "Something will break soon. It always does."

"It better," Alonzo said.

El Sereno left the jet.

Monday, September 5

School starts tomorrow. I have spent the last several days shopping. Incredibly, my arms and legs have outgrown the clothes I bought just last spring. If this continues I'll be called Spider Boy. Mom offered to drive me to Salt Lake City, where there are better choices, but I told her I could make do with Elko duds. She needs to get her store open and has better things to do than haul me around.

The best thing I found shopping was a black leather backpack that's just the right size for my journal, pencils, and a few books. It was kind of expensive, but Mom took pity on me and let me buy it.

I'm nervous about school. I haven't started in a new school since I was in kindergarten. Back then I didn't know enough to be nervous. Now I'll be the new kid and I don't know how to do that.

* * *

Zach sat across the cluttered desk of the principal of Elko Middle School, Mrs. Pyle. She was a heavyset woman with red hair and reading glasses balanced on the end of her nose.

"Is that Z-A-C-K, Z-A-C, Z-A-K, or Z-A-C-H?" Mrs. Pyle asked.

Zach didn't know. He had never seen his new name spelled out. He stalled for time. "Is this a test?"

Wrong answer. Mrs. Pyle's eyes narrowed and her lips tighten into a frown. "No, it is not a test," she said stiffly. "Which is it?"

"Z-A-C-K," he guessed.

Mrs. Pyle opened the thick envelope his mother had given him and shook out a pile of paper onto her desk. Among the papers were Zach's fake transcripts. He hoped they had improved his grades. Mrs. Pyle examined one of the papers and her frowned deepened. Guess they hadn't improved them, Zach thought. "Are you trying to be funny?" she asked.

"I beg your pardon?"

She dropped the sheet in front of him. It was a copy of his new birth certificate. *Zachary Colin Granger*, it said. Colin? Zach thought.

"Z-A-C-H," she informed him. "Short for Zachary."

It went downhill from there.

"Where did you move from?" she asked.

"Portland, Oregon." Zach gave her the abbreviated version of his bogus history.

"I used to live in Portland," she said. "Where did you live?"

Zach had never been to Portland and had no idea where

he was supposed to have lived. So much for the weeks of indoctrination. Aunt Doris and Uncle Don should have thought of this. "We moved around a lot," he replied lamely.

Mrs. Pyle didn't like this answer either, but she didn't pursue it. She picked up another piece of paper. "Your parents are divorced?"

Zach nodded, hoping this did not come true.

"Is your father still in Portland?"

Zach's next lie was interrupted by the bell.

"Here's your class schedule." Mrs. Pyle handed him a sheet of paper. Zach stood up. "We have one thousand one hundred and twenty-two students, nearly three hundred more students than we can hold comfortably. The point is, Zach, you are not the only transfer student, and you aren't the only student with divorced parents. I think if you give us a chance here you'll discover that you've landed in a pretty decent place."

Zach's first class was PE. Nothing like starting the day in a locker room with a bunch of naked guys you've never met before, Zach muttered to Commander IF. They issued him gym clothes. He took his clothes off and put them in an empty locker. Commander IF complained about being shut up in the locker, but Zach didn't have a choice. His shirt and gym shorts didn't have pockets. There was a lot of towel snapping and general horsing around. Zach was used to this. What he wasn't used to was not participating himself. No one seemed to notice him.

They filed into the gym, and the PE instructor had them line up.

"I'm Mr. Dugan," the instructor said. "When I call your name, raise your hand." As he called out the names he checked them off on his clipboard.

"Okay, are there any names I didn't call out?"

Zach raised his hand.

Mr. Dugan stood in front of him. "Your name?"

"Zach Granger."

Mr. Dugan checked his clipboard. "You're not on my list. Are you sure you have PE first period?"

Zach nodded.

"You're tall for a seventh grader."

Zach felt everyone's eyes on him.

"Let's see your schedule."

"It's in my locker."

"Well, go get it."

When Zach returned with the schedule, the class was doing laps around the gym.

"Counterclockwise!" Mr. Dugan shouted. He stood in the middle making notes on his clipboard. Zach broke through the circle and handed him the schedule. Mr. Dugan looked it over, then wrote his name on the clipboard. "You play basketball, Zach?"

"No," Zach said.

"What a waste." It seemed to Zach he was disappointing everyone today. "Clockwise!" Mr. Dugan shouted. The group reversed direction. "Well, get moving, Zach. Or can't you run, either?"

Not very well, Zach thought. The pins and screws in his legs gave him trouble if he put too much stress on them.

"Okay run in place! Lift those knees! Go! Go! Go! Use those legs. . . ."

When Jack had gotten out of the hospital he couldn't walk. Neil Osborne would not accept this. He wheeled Jack into their daylight basement, which he had converted into a gym while Jack was in the hospital. There were weights, punching bags, jump ropes, and in the center of it all, a small boxing ring.

"What's this?" Jack asked.

"I'm going to teach you how to box."

"Hard to do from a wheelchair, Dad."

"We'll get you out of that contraption in no time."

"What does boxing have to do with my legs?"

"Eighty percent of boxing is leg work."

Jack stared at his father.

"I quit my job, Jacko. I'm going to stick around home until you're back on your feet."

"You quit flying?"

"Yeah, for the time being. I've been wanting to get out of the commercial airline business for a long time now."

"What are you going to do after I get back on my feet?"

"Buy a small airline company if I can swing it. Go into business for myself."

With the help of a physical therapist and boxing, it had taken nearly a year for Jack to get back on his feet.

After PE Zach showered and followed the herd of sweating bodies to his homeroom. This teacher's name was Ms. Miller. When everyone was seated, she announced that the desk they had chosen would remain their seat for the rest of the year. Zach was relieved that he had found a desk in the back row near the windows. Several other students were not as thrilled with their choice. When the moans over the seating arrangements died down, Ms. Miller said she wanted everyone to stand up in turn and introduce themselves.

"I know many of you know each other, but I want you to act as if you don't," Ms. Miller said. "I'll start. My name is Ms. Miller. I've been a teacher at Elko Middle School for twenty-two years. This will be my last year teaching. Next year at this time, I hope to be sitting on a warm Mexican beach watching whales frolic in the cobalt-blue water. I trust you'll help me make this last year of teaching my best."

One by one the students stood and introduced themselves. Some of them made jokes, some took the exercise seriously. Most of them seemed to know each other. But there were several who were new to the school, like Zach. By the order in which Ms. Miller was calling them, it looked like Zach was going to be the last to be called upon. He was dreading it. Ms. Miller called on the girl sitting in front of him. All Zach could see was her long, shiny black hair and tight blue jeans. I'm next, Zach thought, what will I say?

"My name is Catalin Cristobal," the girl said. "But most of you know me as Cat. I was born and raised in Elko. I don't know what else to say."

Catalin turned around and smiled at Zach. He stared at her like a deer frozen by headlights, unable to turn his head away. The sound of laughter brought the room back into focus. Zach looked around and saw that the laughter was directed at him.

"And last but not least." Ms. Miller beckoned with her hand.

Zach got to his feet awkwardly, his face flushed with embarrassment. Several people commented about his height.

"My name is . . . Zach Granger. We just moved to Elko." He started to sit down.

"Where did you move from?" Ms. Miller asked.

"Portland."

"Oregon or Maine?"

"Oregon." Please don't say you used to live there, Zach thought.

"Welcome to Elko, Zach," Ms. Miller said.

Zach sat down, relieved. He didn't hear much of what Ms. Miller had to say after that. He looked out the window to avoid looking at Catalin's black hair. The lunch bell rang. He went to his locker to dump his books and discovered that Catalin had the locker right next to his. Rather than face her, he carried his books to the cafeteria and pretended to read while he ate.

Friday, September 22

I've been in the school for over two weeks. . . .

Wanda wants the lead role in Sam's opera and her singing is driving me crazy! She has a part-time job waiting tables at a restaurant, and our phone is ringing off the hook. It's never for me. Is Wanda there? Is Wanda there? Is Wanda there?

I haven't gotten a single phone call since we moved here. I don't know what it is, but I can't seem to make myself talk to anyone at school. I think it has something to do with the fact that I can't tell them the truth about who I am.

Pitiful! I'm sure my classmates are referring to me as the tall snob by now. I need to get past this, but it's getting harder and harder as the days go by. No offence, Commander IF, but I need some taller friends.

*   *   *

Zach was shy around new people. But in his old school this hadn't been a problem. He had known everyone there since kindergarten. He wished he were more like his father, who could step into a room full of complete strangers and have a half dozen lifelong friends by the time he left. If the constant phone calls were any indication, Wanda seemed to have inherited this trait.

Today I am going to make a new friend, he told himself on the way to school. Who? Commander IF asked.

"I don't know, but I'm going to get it out of the way first thing. I'll do it during PE."

But Zach didn't. He told himself that it would be better to make friends with someone in his homeroom. Maybe Catalin Cristobal. No, Commander IF said. Too ambitious. Start small and work your way up. The minutes ticked by. The bell rang, and still he hadn't talked to anyone.

Lunch, Zach told himself. I'll make a friend at lunch. In the cafeteria he got his food and sat at the end of a table near some guys from his PE class. No one spoke to him. He got a book out and started to read.

Science class, he thought. That's when I'll do it. The science teacher, Mr. Gibbons, ran a laid-back class and everyone was pretty relaxed. But when the class ended, Zach still hadn't opened his mouth. Thoroughly disgusted with himself, Zach walked to his locker to retrieve his English book for the final class of the day. There was a group of eighth graders clustered around it.

"Excuse me," Zach said, trying to push through the group.

"Can't you see we're talking here?" one of the eighth graders asked. They were not talking; they were leering at Catalin Cristobal, who was getting something out of her locker.

"I'll only be a second."

The eighth grader glared at him. "My name is Peter Short."

Zach had seen him lurking in the hallways. "Congratulations, Peter. I need to get something out of my locker, so if you don't mind . . ."

"Get it later."

"Let him get into his locker, Peter," Catalin said. "Quit being such a jerk."

Zach was not thrilled about having a girl come to his rescue. Especially the girl he wanted to impress. Peter continued to lean against Zach's locker.

"Look." Zach sighed. "I just need to get something out of my locker, then you can resume your position."

"You're new here, aren't you?" Peter asked.

Here was Zach's opportunity. *Yes, I am. My name is Zachary Colin Granger. It's a great honor to meet you, Peter.* "So what," Zach said instead.

"Well, new guy," Peter informed him. "I'm talking to Cat right now and you're bugging me. So, go away before I swat you."

Peter's friends laughed.

"Peter, you're such an idiot!" Catalin shouted, then shoved him.

Peter shoved her back and suddenly something snapped inside Zach. He wasn't exactly sure what happened next, but when it was over, Peter was on the floor and Zach was standing over him with clenched fists. There was a nasty-looking red welt under Peter's left eye and Zach's right hand was throbbing.

"I saw that, Zachary Granger!" the principal, Mrs. Pyle, shouted.

"It wasn't his fault," Catalin pleaded.

"I saw the whole thing, Catalin," Mrs. Pyle said. "Now, you just go to your next class." She looked around at the crowd that had gathered. "In fact, all of you go to your classes, right now. Go!" Everyone scurried away, leaving Zach and Peter alone in the hallway with Mrs. Pyle. Peter was still sprawled on the floor. "Stand up, Peter," Mrs. Pyle said.

He got slowly to his feet. "I was just standing there and he hauled off and hit me in the face. What's the matter with him, Mrs. Pyle?"

"Oh please." Zach rolled his eyes.

"Both of you shut your traps," Mrs. Pyle barked. "Peter, go down to the nurse's room and have one of the secretaries put an ice pack on your eye."

"Yes, ma'am," Peter said sweetly.

She looked at Zach. "You come with me."

"That's not what happened," Zach said, following her.

"You know, Zach, I don't really care why it happened. We don't allow fistfights in our school. Period. I might just suspend you for this. We'll see what Mr. Sebesta has to say."

"The custodian?" Zach had seen Sam around the school, but he hadn't talked to him since that first day. What did Sam have to do with suspending people?

Mrs. Pyle led him to a small door in the back of the

auditorium. "Wait here." She disappeared through the door and reappeared five minutes later.

"He's ready for you."

"I don't understand. What does Sam . . ."

"Just go in!" Mrs. Pyle said irritably. "Mr. Sebesta will bring you to the office when he's finished."

Finished with what? Zach thought as he stepped nervously into the dimly lit, narrow corridor running beneath the stage. At the end of the corridor was an open door with a bright light shining through it.

"Come on in," Sam called.

Zach walked toward the light.

Sam was sitting on a scarred but tidy workbench with his feet dangling over the edge. He was wearing the same khaki work clothes and boots he had been wearing on the day they had met. With the exception of the workbench, the room was not your normal custodial room. It was huge, taking up the entire area beneath the stage. On the ceiling were several trapdoors with large numbers stenciled on them. A heavy punching bag was suspended near one of the trapdoors with a chain. Zach had spent a lot of time in front of a bag just like it after he had fallen from the window. Next to the punching bag was a weight set, which explained the muscles in Sam's arms and chest. Above the long workbench was a shelf filled with books, CDs, and an expensive-looking stereo system. At the far end of the bench was a leather recliner. Standing above the recliner was a lifesize mannequin wearing a full-length black cape and a mask. Zach stared at The Phantom. He was reminded of his caped-crusader days.

"That's The Phantom's costume for the opera," Sam explained.

Zach glanced around the workshop. "Eric lived beneath the Paris Opera house. Your room is beneath the school theater."

"That's right, but there's no underground lake. At least not that I know of."

"I don't understand why Mrs. Pyle brought me down here."

Sam smiled. "Let me see your hands."

"What for?" The last person who had asked to see Zach's hands had been Agent Pelton, and that had not gone well.

"Just hold them up for a second."

Zach did.

"Big hands." Sam jumped off the workbench and opened a cupboard underneath the workbench. He pulled out a pair of boxing gloves. "Try these on for size."

"I'm not going to box with you."

"From what Mrs. Pyle said about your right cross, I don't want to box with you either. You might knock me out." He handed Zach the gloves. "Just put them on."

"Why?"

Sam walked over to the punching bag and slapped it with his hand. "Before we talk, I want you to beat up the bag for a few minutes. Gets rid of the tension. Over the years, half the boys in this school, and some of the girls too, have been in here to have it out with my bag. Your friend Peter has been in here more than a dozen times."

"He's not my friend."

"I gathered that. Put the gloves on."

Zach slipped both gloves on and tightened the laces with his teeth.

Sam raised his eyebrows. "I see you've had gloves on before."

Zach held the gloves out for Sam to tie. "How do they feel?"

"They're a little small."

"Do you know the routine?"

Zach nodded.

Sam got behind the bag and held it steady. "Whale away."

Zach's first punch was a halfhearted attempt that barely moved the bag.

"You can do better than that!"

Zach's second punch was harder.

"You're getting there. Think about your friend Peter."

Whack. Whack.

"Think about being uprooted from your home and friends against your will."

Zach looked at Sam, wondering if he knew more about his situation that he should. Impossible. *Whack. Whack. Whack.*

"Think about anything that makes you really mad, push the anger down your arms into your fists, and slam it into this bag."

Dad, Zach thought. *Whack. Whack. Whack.*

Sam had to lean all his weight into the bag to stop it from swinging. Until that moment Zach hadn't realized he was angry at his father. How could he do this to us? *Whack. Whack.* He didn't just abandon us, he made us abandon our lives, our identities. *Whack.*

Wanda! *Whack*. She has new friends, a job, goals, and a future. *Whack. Whack*. Mom. Leaving Dad to rot in that jail. *Whack*. Her bookstore. Her new life. *Whack. Whack*. And the men who came to visit us that night. Zach stared at the bag. His arms hanging. His chest heaving. The men. I did nothing to stop them. They could have killed us. The men who might still kill us. *Whack. Whack. Whack* . . . He punched the bag until he could not longer lift his arms. It wasn't until he stopped, gasping for breath, that he realized he was crying. He felt the gloves being unlaced and saw Sam's face in a blur of tears. Sam guided Zach over to the recliner and sat him down. A moment later he felt a glass of water being put into his swollen hand.

"Drink it."

Zach had to hold the glass with both hands so he didn't drop it. His arms shook as he brought the glass up to his mouth. Sam brought him a towel. Zach wiped the sweat and tears off his face with the realization that something remarkable had just taken place. Rather than feeling embarrassed about breaking down in front of a complete stranger, Zach felt good. Calmness flowed through his body. He felt light, as if he were floating above the recliner.

"That was quite a session," Sam said, pulling a stool up in front of the recliner.

"What was that all about?" Zach asked.

"How do you feel?"

Zach smiled. "I feel good. Relieved, I guess."

Sam nodded. "That was about anger, Zach. I saw it in you the first time we met."

"I wasn't angry then."

91

"Yes, you were. And I thought you might be in here having a session with the bag before too long." He laughed. "Didn't expect it this soon though."

"You say that a lot of other guys have been in here?"

"Not this year. Yet. But over the years a number of them have paid the bag a visit. Sometimes Mrs. Pyle brings them down, sometimes a teacher does, and sometimes they just come on their own before they get in trouble."

"In my other school the vice principal was in charge of discipline. If that's what this was."

"We used to have a vice principal here who filled that role. He didn't have a bag, though. I took over when he left. We have a new vice principal now, but Mrs. Pyle liked the results so much she asked me to continue. Sometimes you've got to let it all out before you can sit down and really talk about it. Are you ready to talk about what's bothering you?"

"Peter was standing in front of my locker." Zach didn't want to involve Catalin. "When I tried to open it he got in my face. I guess I just blew up."

"I think there's a lot more to it than that." Sam stared at him, waiting for an answer.

A *lot* more, Zach thought, but he couldn't tell Sam. He couldn't talk about it to anyone. What's happening to me? In my old school I was never in serious trouble. Now I'm about ready to be suspended.

"It was just one of those things," Zach said. "It won't happen again. Will I be suspended?"

Sam's eyes continued to stare at him for a moment, then gave him an odd grin. "That's up to Mrs. Pyle."

"She said that it was up to you."

"Custodians can't suspend people," Sam laughed. "Have you made any friends here?"

Zach shook his head.

"Yes, you have."

"I don't understand."

"There's me for one. I know that I may not be exactly what you have in mind when you think of a friend, but you're welcome to come by here anytime."

"For the bag?"

"If you like. But you could just come by here to say hello or just to talk."

"Thanks."

"School's out." Sam nodded toward the clock on the wall. Zach hadn't even heard the bell. "We better go by Mrs. Pyle's office and find out what the verdict is."

Zach waited outside Mrs. Pyle's office while Sam went inside to talk to her. When Sam came out, he winked and told Zach to go in. Mrs. Pyle said that she had talked to Peter's parents, and it was lucky for Zach they weren't upset about the fight.

"Peter's going to have a nice shiner by Monday morning," she said. "He's been known to give a few himself in the past, and it would probably be best to stay clear of him."

"Am I suspended?"

"No. I'm going to let you off this time, but if I ever catch you fighting with a classmate again, you're out of here. And I won't care what they did to deserve it."

"Thank you."

"You can thank Mr. Sebesta. I was ready to suspend you, but he talked me out of it." She stood up. "You can go now."

Zach started to leave.

"One more thing," Mrs. Pyle said, stopping him in his tracks. "Sam said you were a smart kid, a reader. He told me you had even read *Phantom of the Opera.* Is that true?"

Zach nodded.

"Well, keep your nose in a book and out of Peter Short's face and you won't have any more problems here."

When Zach left the building, he found Catalin sitting at the bottom of the stairs reading a book. She closed it when she saw him and put it into her backpack.

"Peter is a jerk," she told him.

"I shouldn't have hit him."

"Maybe not." She pulled something from her backpack. "I think you dropped this."

Commander IF was in the palm of her hand. His tiny helmeted head had been severed and was lying next to his body.

"You might be able to glue the head back on," Catalin said casually, as if everyone in the school owned a tiny wooden astronaut. "It must have gotten stepped on when you hit Peter."

Zach stared at Commander IF in shock. He wasn't upset that he had lost his head. He was upset that Catalin had him in her hand. "It's not mine." He hated himself for saying it, but he wasn't going to admit to Catalin that he carried a toy astronaut in his pocket who was his imaginary friend.

"Really? I could have sworn that it dropped out of your pocket."

"Not likely."

"I guess I was mistaken." Catalin slipped Commander IF

into her backpack and started to walk away, then stopped and looked back. "Zach, I like the color of your eyes."

Blue lies, Zach thought. He watched her until she turned the corner.

11

Sunday, September 24

I can't believe that I abandoned Commander IF! But what else could I have done? "Thanks for picking up my imaginary friend, Catalin. Are you impressed? Do you want to hang out with a guy whose best friend—whose only friend—is an inch-and-a-half long toy astronaut?"

And speaking of friends . . . My first genuine contact with a classmate was a right cross to his face! Not that Peter Short and I would have ever become friends, but this is not what I had in mind when I woke up last Friday. I wonder if Jack would have done the same when I was him. Probably not. Jack would have walked away from the situation—shown up in English class without his book and told the teacher he had forgotten it.

Mrs. Pyle has not called Mom. Yet. And I'm not going to tell her about Peter unless I have to. She has enough to worry about. I just need to calm down and try to keep the feeling I had after my session in Sam's lair beneath the stage.

Catalin has been on my mind all weekend. I wonder where she lives. And what she really meant by liking the color of my eyes.

We ran errands this weekend. On Saturday we looked at cars for Wanda so she can drive to work and school without Mom having to chauffeur her. We found a used Honda without too many miles on it and today we drove it all the way to Salt Lake where Mom looked at computers. She couldn't decide which one to buy, so we drove all the way there for nothing.

On the way to school Monday, Zach was less concerned about making new friends. The calmness that had come after beating the heavy bag still remained, although his arms and legs were sore. When he walked up the stairs to the school several people said hello to him. He tried not to act too surprised and pleased, but he was both. When he got inside the first thing he did was look for Peter, who was not hard to find. He was standing in the hallway surrounded by half a dozen students admiring his black eye, which was the color and size of a charcoal briquette. When Zach walked up to Peter, the groupies stepped aside.

"I'm sorry about the eye." Zach held his hand out.

Peter looked at Zach's hand for a second then said, "You couldn't have touched me if I'd been expecting it."

"You're probably right. No hard feelings?"

"We'll see." Peter did not take Zach's hand.

Zach's next stop was the custodial room, but Sam wasn't there. After a short search he found Sam in the boys' locker room, filling the soap dispensers.

"Morning, Zach."

"Thanks for helping me out on Friday."

Sam shrugged his shoulders. "It was no big deal."

"I apologized to Peter."

"Really? And how did Peter take it?"

"I'm not sure."

"Well, I'd stay clear of him and his minions for a while. He's going to be thinking about what you did to him every time he looks in the mirror."

Zach was relieved to discover that Catalin was out sick. He had been thinking about telling her that the astronaut was his. Now he had another day to reconsider. During lunch a couple of guys from his homeroom sat next to him and he managed to have an actual conversation. One of them, Darrell Gill, lived a block from the Grangers and invited Zach over to his house.

"I'll give you a call after dinner," Darrell said.

When Zach got home from school he was surprised to find his mother there cleaning the house. Wanda was at work.

"Give me a hand," Mrs. Granger said. "A contractor is coming over tonight to give me a bid for the carpentry work in the bookstore. How about putting the dishes in the washer for me?"

Zach started to load it up.

"How was school?"

"Good," Zach said. And this time he meant it. "Who's the contractor?"

"A nice old guy. I checked his references today and everyone says that he's the best in town for this kind of job, and he's very reasonable. Apparently, he has a couple of Basques working for him, and they're supposed to be excellent carpenters."

Halfway through dinner the phone rang. "It's probably for Wanda," Mrs. Granger said.

"You never know." Zach picked it up. It was Darrell. When he hung up he told his mother he was going over to a friend's house for a while.

She smiled. "I want you home by nine at the latest."

Zach smiled back. It had been a long time since he had heard that. Too long.

Darrell's father opened the front door of a house that wasn't much bigger than Zach's. Mr. Gill had red hair like his son, but that was where the similarity ended. He wore his hair in a crew cut, not down to his shoulders as Darrell did. He was a big man with a large belly spilling over his belt. Darrell was small and could probably wear one of his father's pant legs as a skirt.

"You the kid that socked Peter Short in the eye?" Mr. Gill asked.

Zach wished Darrell had not told his dad. "I guess so."

"Good! Come on in."

The inside of the Gills' house was set up exactly like the Grangers'. Mrs. Gill was sitting on a loveseat in the living/dining/family room staring at a big-screen television. Next to her was the smallest poodle Zach had ever seen. It looked like a squirrel with black curly hair. Neither Mrs. Gill nor the poodle looked away from the screen when Zach walked in. There was a deodorant commercial on.

"Darrell's in his room." Mr. Gill pointed to a door that would have been Zach's if he had been in his own house.

"Thanks," Zach said.

Mr. Gill joined his wife and the poodle on the loveseat. Zach knocked on the bedroom door. No one answered. He opened the door and saw Darrell sitting on the end of his bed in front of a television screen with a video game controller in his hands, and headphones clamped over his ears. The bedroom was the same size as Zach's, but the decor was different. The walls were covered with photos of Darrell posing with dead animals, targets with bullet holes in them, and pictures torn from hunting magazines. The bedspread was made out of camouflage material. So were the pillowcases. G.I. Darrell, Zach thought.

The game ended and Darrell slipped the headphones off. "You play?"

"Sure," Zach said, although this was not exactly true—which became obvious after Darrell blew Zach to pieces twenty-six times in eleven minutes.

Darrell switched the television off. "I guess video games aren't your thing. Do you hunt?"

"You mean animals?"

"Duh."

"No," Zach said. "But I'm not against hunting."

"Do you fish?"

"No."

"But you aren't against it?"

Zach grinned. "Right."

"So, what do you like to do?"

"I don't know. I guess I like to read."

"So I've noticed. In fact, everyone at the school has noticed. No one in the history of Elko Middle School has read a book during lunch. It's not natural. What are you trying to prove?"

Zach wasn't trying to prove anything, but he knew he had to come up with a decent answer or risk losing Darrell as a potential friend. "Cafeteria food is a lot easier to swallow if you don't look at it while you are putting it in your mouth," Zach said. "Reading keeps my eyes off the slop on the tray."

Darrell laughed. "I knew it was something like that! The other guys thought you were some kind of geek, but I told them I thought there was more to you than that. You proved my point when you punched Peter out."

"That isn't why I did it."

"Peter deserved it. He hassles everyone. The only people who like him are the three stooges who hang out with him. Did you go down to Sam's torture chamber and punch the bag?"

"Yeah. Have you ever been down there?"

Darrell nodded. "A few times. Sam's a weird dude, but I like him. I bet Peter Short's been down there a hundred times. He's always getting in trouble or causing trouble for someone else."

"Your dad doesn't seem very fond of Peter either."

"My dad doesn't even know Peter. His problem is with Peter's dad."

"What does he have against Peter's dad?"

"I don't know all the details, but he used to work for my dad at the mine. A couple years ago, Mr. Short came up with

101

a get-rich-quick scheme, and a lot of the miners bought into it. Everyone, including my dad, lost their money except for Mr. Short. He quit his job at the mine and started dropping piles of money at the Nugget Casino, eventually losing everything. Some of the miners tried to sue him, but all he had left was the old trailer they live in at the trailer park. Most people thought the Shorts would move on, but they stayed."

"Where does he work now?" Zach asked.

"Nowhere, really. He's a hustler. Runs private poker games for high rollers from out of town. He and Peter's mom spend whatever he gets in the casinos. He's always working an angle. Peter's the same way. Like father, like son, I guess."

Zach thought about his own father shackled to the floor in an orange jumpsuit and had an extremely uncomfortable moment.

"Peter and me used to be friends in grade school, but things change. So, what do you do when you're not reading a book?"

Zach decided not to tell him about his interest in museums. He liked Darrell, despite their differences, and he wanted to see where the friendship would go. "Nothing much lately. I guess I'm trying to adjust to life in Elko. I've never lived in a small town."

"I've lived here my whole life," Darrell said. "Did you know that Elko has three E's?"

"What do you mean?"

"Everyone knows Everything about Everybody. For instance, my dad knew that you slugged Peter in the eye

102

with a right cross before I got home from school."

"You're kidding."

"He heard about it at the mine. And if my dad heard about it, everyone in Elko has heard about it. What did your mom say?"

"She doesn't know. I didn't tell her about it."

"Mrs. Pyle didn't call her?"

Zach shook his head. He was surprised at this too. "So, maybe Elko doesn't have three—"

Darrell interrupted him. "How much money do you have on you?"

"Why?"

"Just count it."

Zach emptied his pockets. He had $3.58.

"Okay," Darrell said. "I'll bet you three fifty-eight that she hears about it before Friday."

"I can't believe that it's as bad as that."

"Is it a bet?"

"And you won't tell her?"

"I won't have to."

They shook on it and Zach went home wondering if Darrell had just hustled him.

Parked outside Zach's house was an old truck with a dented canopy. Zach assumed it belonged to the contractor. But what kind of contractor would drive a truck like that? He went into the house.

"We're in here," his mother called.

Zach took the five steps to the kitchen door.

"This is—" Mrs. Granger began.

"Sam!" Zach stared at the custodian in confusion. He

was certain that he had just lost $3.58 to Darrell Gill.

"You know each other?" Mrs. Granger asked, acting as surprised at Zach was.

"I'm the custodian at Zach's school," Sam explained.

Zach looked at his mother. She seemed in pretty good spirits, which would not be the case if Sam had told her about the fight with Peter Short. Maybe I don't owe Darrell $3.58, he thought. Yet.

"You're a contractor?" Zach asked.

"Part-time." Sam turned to Zach's mother. "I have a confession, Mrs. Granger." Here it comes, Zach thought. "I met your son a few days before school started and he told me that you were opening a bookstore."

"So, your dropping by the store last week wasn't a coincidence," Mrs. Granger said.

"No." Sam smiled. "Small contracts like this are hard to find."

Mrs. Granger smiled back at him. "Well, we don't have a contract yet. You still haven't told me how much all of this is going to cost."

Sam took a small notebook out of his shirt pocket. "I've already done some figuring. I think I can get it done for seven to eight thousand dollars."

Mrs. Granger laughed in relief. "I thought it would cost a lot more than that."

"Actually," Sam said, "I was thinking of knocking a bit off the price."

"I don't see how you could."

"What I had in mind was a little exchange of labor." He glanced at Zach. "It's up to you and Zach of course, but I just

104

bought the building next door to where I live, and it needs a good cleaning. I thought you might be interested, Zach. The pay is good, and on the days you work, dinner's included. I'll knock off five hundred dollars from the total, Mrs. Granger. That is, if you and Zach agree."

She looked at Zach. "What do you think?"

"It's okay with me," Zach said. "But who gets the five hundred?"

"I'll give you half and put the other half in your college account."

Zach grinned. "Then it's a deal, Sam." They shook hands on it.

"One more thing," Mrs. Granger said. "How soon can you be done with the bookstore, Mr. Sebesta? I've already started ordering books, and I want to open by November if possible."

"We'll have it done by the middle of October. Maybe sooner."

Mrs. Granger wrote him a check.

Later that night, Mrs. Granger asked Zach and Wanda into the living/dining/family room for a family meeting.

"It's been seven weeks since those men came," she began. "I'm wondering how you're feeling now. I know this whole situation is strange, but do you both feel safe now?"

"I think I do," Wanda said carefully. "But maybe I've been too busy to think about it. Elko's not as bad as I thought it would be."

"How about you, Zach?"

"I feel okay. What happened to us seems sort of like a dream now. Are you going to send the postcard?"

"I'm thinking about it. Dad won't do anything about his situation until he knows we're safe."

"If he gets out, will he come live with us?" Zach asked.

"I don't know," she said quietly.

Friday, September 29

I'm writing this in the cafeteria. Darrell is sitting across the table from me reading a hunting magazine. I tried to get him to read a book, but he told me not to push my luck. A few other people are reading too, including Catalin and a couple of her girlfriends, three tables away. I don't think they are reading hunting magazines.

I haven't talked to Peter since I apologized to him last week, but I've caught him watching me as if he's sizing me up. It kind of gives me the creeps, which is what he's probably trying to do. His eye looks a little better.

I think Wanda and Mom are actually beginning to like living in Elko. I can't say I like it yet, but it is growing on me. Last night, Mom sat Wanda and me down and asked us if we thought it was safe. The postcard was still on the refrigerator when I left for school this morning. . . .

The bell rang. Darrell looked up from his hunting magazine. "I hope you don't expect me to start writing during lunch too."

"Maybe next year," Zach joked. "After you graduate from magazines to real books."

"Very funny. Why don't you come over tomorrow and we can have another go at the video games. I'll use my toes this time so you'll have a chance of winning."

Zach laughed. "Can't do it. I start my job for Sam tomorrow." He put the journal into his backpack. "By the way, it's the end of the week and my mom hasn't said one thing to me about Peter Short. I think you owe me three fifty-eight."

Darrell gave Zach $3.60. "You owe me two cents," he said.

When Zach got home from school he went directly to the refrigerator to get something to eat. The space shuttle postcard had taken off.

On Saturday morning Zach met Sam at the bookstore. Sam's two Basque carpenters were named Iker and Jakome Mateo. Sam told them he would be back as soon as he got Zach started on the building.

Sam drove him downtown and pulled up in front of a hotel.

"Why are we stopping here?" Zach asked.

"Because this is where I live."

"You live in a hotel?"

"Oh this is not just any hotel. This is the Nevada Hotel. Do you know anything about the Basques?"

"A little." Zach told Sam what he had learned about the Basques at the museum.

"The Basques are the greatest people on earth. You'll find that out for yourself if you hang out at the Nevada long enough. It's owned and operated by Basques. My terrible building is right next door."

Zach followed him into a dilapidated building. Sam was not exaggerating. The inside of the building was a disaster. A thick layer of wood sawdust covered every square inch including the walls and windowpanes.

"What was this place?" Zach asked.

"They used to make furniture in here."

"I think you should have knocked off a thousand dollars from Mom's contract," Zach said.

Sam laughed. "You just learned your first lesson as an independent contractor. Never bid on a job until after you've seen it."

"I'll keep that in mind."

"I've got garbage bags, brooms, dustpans—everything you'll need to get started. I'm going back to the bookstore to help Iker and Jakome. We only have a few weeks to get the job done. I'll come back around dinner time."

In his previous life Zach had not done much manual labor aside from cleaning his room, helping his father in the woodshop once in a while, and occasional yard work. The first thing he did was to wipe the dust off the windows so he could see what he was doing. This caused a whirlwind of swirling, choking dust that drove him hacking and coughing out of the building.

There was so much dust billowing out the door, Zach

was afraid someone might mistake it for smoke and call the fire department. It took nearly half an hour for the dust to settle enough for him to venture back inside. He opened the windows, which seemed to help, and spent the rest of the day filling thirty-seven plastic bags with sawdust, which hardly made a dent in the mess.

Sam returned while Zach was filling the thirty-eighth bag. "It's hard to tell you apart from the dirt inside. Your hair looks like a dust mop. Are you hungry?"

"I don't know." Zach laughed. "My stomach's filled with sawdust."

"You better come with me, but we'll have to get you a shower before we feed you. I hope the drain doesn't plug."

Zach followed him outside and brushed off as much sawdust as he could before they went into the Nevada.

"We'll go in the back way," Sam said. "Don't want to scare the dinner crowd."

"It's a restaurant too?"

"You'll see."

Zach followed him up a narrow set of stairs to the second floor.

"Why don't you take your clothes off here in the hallway. And don't worry, we don't have any female boarders at the moment, so you're safe. The shower is through that door. While you're rinsing off, I'll see what I can do about finding you a clean set of clothes. You're just about Iker's size. He should have something you can wear."

Zach piled his dusty clothes in the hallway, then took a long hot shower. The drain got plugged with sludge twice, but he managed to clear it. When he stepped out of the stall there was a pile of clean clothes on the chair. The pants were too big in the waist and too short in the legs, but they would get him through dinner.

Zach stepped out into the hallway. Sam was waiting for him.

"I just took your clothes downstairs," he said. "They'll have them washed by the time dinner's over." He looked at his watch. "And dinner will be ready soon. You can wait in my room while I take a shower."

Zach followed him down the hallway, past doors with numbers painted on them. Sam lived behind door number eight. The room was very simple. There was a single bed, neatly made, a small closet, and a sturdy table with piles of magazines and newspapers. Above the table was a bookcase stuffed with books.

"I hope you saved me some hot water." Sam took some clothes from the closet and told Zach that he would be right back.

Zach looked out the room's only window. Not much to see. Across the street was a small grocery store. On the next street over were the bright flashing lights of the Nugget Casino. Why did Sam live in a hotel? Zach didn't know how much money custodians made, but with his contracting business, Sam could certainly afford to live in a house. As Zach looked around the room he noticed there wasn't anything hanging on the walls. In fact, there wasn't a single photograph in the room, which seemed odd to Zach. Even the Grangers had photographs of their past lives.

He sat down at the table and picked up a magazine about opera. He put it down and picked up another magazine. It was written in a foreign language that Zach thought might be Russian. What was Sam doing with this? He got up and started looking at the books in the case. Some were written in the same alphabet as the magazine and a couple other books appeared to be written in Arabic. The door opened and Sam came in rubbing his gray hair with a towel.

Zach pulled a book off the shelf. "What language is this written in?"

"Russian."

"You can read Russian?"

"I used to be able to," Sam said, hanging the towel on the rack attached to the closet door. "Pretty rusty now."

"How about this book?" Zach pulled out one of the Arabic books.

"Oh that," Sam dismissed it. "A lifetime ago I had a roommate from Saudi Arabia."

"How long have you been in Elko?"

"Twelve years." He combed his hair in the mirror.

"Where were you before?"

"Here and there." A loud bell clanged from somewhere in the hotel. "Dinner! I hope you worked up an appetite. Have you ever eaten Basque food?"

"I don't think so."

"Then you're in for a treat."

Zach followed Sam out into the hallway where they joined a group of men making their way down the stairs. The men spoke in what Zach assumed was Basque with a smattering of English words thrown in. Sam joined in the friendly banter.

"You speak Basque too?" Zach asked.

"A little."

At the bottom of the stairs was a large empty room with framed black-and-white photographs hanging on the walls. Zach had seen some of the same photos at the Northeastern Nevada Museum. Most of the photos were taken in sheep camps up in the mountains. Sam was in a couple of them.

"How often do you go up to the sheep camps?" Zach asked.

"Several times a year," Sam said. "I'll take you up with me sometime if you want."

"I'd like that."

Outside the gallery was a bar with several men sitting on stools drinking. A few of them got up and followed Sam and Zach into the dining room, where they joined the other men at a long table filled with platters of several kinds of meat, salad, spaghetti, beans, bread, butter, pitchers of iced tea, water, and coffee. Zach sat down next to Sam near the end of the table and the men started passing the food around and heaping it onto their plates.

There were several other smaller tables situated around the big table with couples and families sitting at them. A smaller version of the Basques' feast was at each table.

"We're served dinner like this every night," Sam said, helping himself to the salad. "The small tables are for locals and tourists. They come in here when the dinner bell sounds to watch the boarders chow down."

The last pork chop was forked off the platter just as it got to Zach. Before he could show his disappointment another platter of pork chops appeared over his shoulder. Zach turned.

"Hi, Zach."

It was Catalin. By the time he had gotten over his shock at seeing her there, she had moved away with the empty platter and disappeared into the kitchen.

"I see you know Catalin Cristobal," Sam said.

"She's in my homeroom, but I didn't know she worked here."

"Her father and mother own the place. Catalin's been helping out here since she could walk."

Catalin came back out of the kitchen with a bowl of salad and platter of meat for one of the other tables. As she moved across the room she gave Zach a small smile. Zach returned it, and nearly choked on the hunk of meat he was chewing.

Sam grinned. "Catalin is a nice-looking girl."

Zach changed the subject. "Why do you live in a hotel?"

"I'm a bachelor. My room is cleaned every day, my laundry is washed for me, and of course there's the food."

"What do the other boarders do?" Zach asked.

"Some of them work at the gold mine, others are sheep herders down from the hills for a little rest and relaxation. Iker and Jakome work full-time for me. They've been here a little less than a year. They came over to earn enough money to buy a sheep ranch of their own back in the old country."

"Why don't they herd sheep here?"

"There aren't many herding jobs anymore. Doesn't pay that well anyway. They're doing fine as carpenters. I suspect in another year they'll have enough to go home if they still want to."

"What do you mean if they want to?"

"Life here is pretty good. Some of these young guys meet girls who have no interest in going back to the old country. Catalin's grandfather, Benat Pasquale, came over in 1946 with every intention of returning with a bucket full of money, but he never made it back. He herded sheep, saved his money, met Catalin's grandmother, and at her urging, he bought the hotel."

"Does he work here too?"

"No, he spends most of his time up in the hills herding sheep. He doesn't like it in town too much. He thinks it's too crowded."

Zach laughed. "Elko, crowded?"

Sam smiled. "All depends what you're used to, I guess. Anyway, Catalin's grandmother ran the hotel and raised the family while Benat stayed up in the hills. He would come down every month or two to see what was going on, but after a while he started to worry about his sheep and he'd go back up. Catalin's grandmother passed away several years ago, and her parents took over the hotel."

A half hour later the men began pushing their chairs back from the table and leaving. Zach was stuffed.

"I'll take you home," Sam offered. "But first you better retrieve your clothes. Catalin should know where they are. You can come up to my room and change."

Zach walked into the kitchen to find Catalin.

"Can I help you?" a woman asked. She had the same color hair and same smile as Catalin. It had to be her mother.

"My name's Zach Granger. I'm looking for my clothes."

"I've heard about you, Zach," she said. "Your clothes are

115

through there." She pointed at a door in the back of the kitchen. "This is Catalin's father. Adrian?"

A man with thick black hair looked up from the stove where he was frying meat and came over wiping his hands on a towel.

"This is Zach Granger," Mrs. Cristobal said. "The one Catalin has been talking about."

Zach was pleased to hear this.

"Ah, the mystery boy," Mr. Cristobal exclaimed. "You're new to Elko, I understand."

Zach gave him the story, which was getting a little easier for him to tell.

"And your mother is opening a bookstore."

Elko's three E's, Zach thought. "With Sam and the Mateo brothers' help," he said.

The man flipping meat on the stove yelled something in Basque and Mr. Cristobal hurried over to give him a hand.

"Nice meeting you, Zach," Mrs. Cristobal said. "You are welcome here anytime."

"The food was really great. Thanks."

Mrs. Cristobal picked up two platters heaped with meat and pushed the door to the dining room open with her hip. Zach walked through the back door and found Catalin standing in front of a clothes dryer with her back to him.

"Hi, Catalin."

She gave a little jump and turned around. "You scared me!"

"Sorry."

"Your clothes are still drying."

"I'm not in any hurry."

116

She looked at the clothes Zach was wearing. "Iker's or Jakome's?"

"Iker I think, and they were a lot baggier before I ate."

"The first time you've eaten Basque food?"

"Yeah, and I hope it's not the last."

"Sam said that meals were part of your deal with him."

"I might have offered to do the work for free if I'd known the food would be so good."

They looked at each other, neither one knowing what to say next.

Zach broke the awkward silence. "Do you live here at the hotel?"

"No, we have a house not far from school. In fact, it's only about three blocks from your house."

The three E's again. But in this case, Zach was glad that Catalin knew where he lived.

"Do you work here every day?"

"Just on Friday and Saturday evenings, but I'm here a lot."

This is turning into a pretty good job, Zach thought. Another awkward silence followed, which was broken by Catalin.

"Has Peter given you any more problems?" she asked.
"No."

"Well, you better stay away from him," she warned.

"You're not the first person to tell me that."

"He hasn't been the same since his dad got in trouble."
"How so?"

"For one, he used to be a nice guy. We went to the same grade school."

"Darrell Gill told me about his dad and the get-rich scheme."

"I think it's been a lot harder on Peter than his parents."

"Why have they stayed in town?"

"Peter's mom and dad have the gambling bug bad. Every time they get some money, they blow it all at one of the casinos. It's kind of sad really. They adopted Peter when he was four years old. I'm not sure why. They've never seemed very interested in him. I think Peter would give just about anything to get out of here. I feel sorry for him. We don't get to pick our parents or where we live."

"Or our names," Zach said.

Catalin laughed. "That's right, we don't."

The dryer stopped. Catalin pulled Zach's shirt and pants out. "I guess I better get back to work."

"I appreciate you washing my clothes."

Catalin smiled and walked into the kitchen.

13

Sunday, October 1

I don't have much time to write today because I'm in the middle of cleaning Sam's building. The job is hard, but the pay is good, the food is amazing, and Catalin is about 150 feet from where I'm working.

By Sunday afternoon Zach had managed to get most of the sawdust out of the building, but there was still a lot more to do. Surveying the mess, he figured he would have the building cleaned out about the time he entered high school. He walked across the street to the store and bought a Coke. When he got back, Sam and Catalin were inside the building looking over his work.

"It's starting to look good in here," Sam said. "Now all I

have to do is figure out what to do with that mountain of bagged sawdust outside. Are you ready to take a break?"

"I just did." Zach held up his can of Coke.

"I mean a longer break."

"What about dinner?" Zach asked, but what he was really worried about was missing a chance to spend time with Cat.

"You'll have a Basque dinner," Cat said. "But this time it will be authentic."

"Last night's wasn't?"

"Basque food tastes better when it's cooked in the mountains. We're going to take some supplies up to my grandfather. He'll want to feed us when we get up there. Dinner *and* breakfast. No school tomorrow. Teachers' in-service day."

"We're spending the night up there?"

Sam nodded. "That is if you want to, and if it's okay with your mom."

"Of course I want to."

After a quick shower, Sam drove Zach over to the bookstore to ask his mother. On the way back they stopped at Zach's house to pick up some clothes. And by the time they arrived at the hotel, Catalin and her parents had all the supplies ready for her grandfather.

As the truck pulled away Mrs. Cristobal shouted, "You tell that old bear that we want him down here for a visit in the next two weeks. Or I'm going to send a couple boarders up to haul him down the mountain by force!"

Catalin leaned across Zach and shouted back, "It will take more than a couple of boarders to get the bear off the mountain."

"Who's the bear?" Zach asked.

"My grandfather, Benat Pasquale," Catalin explained. "*Benat* means 'bear' in Basque."

They arrived at the sheep camp near sunset. An old man wearing a weathered cowboy hat, down vest, and woolen pants with cuffs tucked into scuffed cowboy boots walked out of a very large canvas tent. When Zach opened the door to the truck, Catalin nearly climbed over the top of him to get to her grandfather. Benat picked her up under the arms and swung her in a complete circle. A second man came out of the tent and walked over to Sam and Zach.

"This is Benat's partner, Ander Toussaint," Sam said.

Ander smiled at Zach, then began an animated conversation with Sam in Basque. Zach listened for a while, then stepped away and took in his new surroundings. Streaks of red sunlight washed across hundreds of sheep grazing on the steep hillside beyond the tent. A cool, light breeze buffeted the white smoke coming from the tent's stovepipe. About fifty feet from the camp was a small corral made of rough-cut trees. Tied to the top rails were two saddled horses. Zach walked over to get a closer look at them. He had never ridden a horse. His parents' idea of a vacation had not included horses, camping, or anything remotely related to the outdoors. When the Osbornes had gone on vacation, they visited cities, theme parks, and museums, and they stayed in hotels. This was another reason Zach was surprised his mother had chosen to move to Elko, Nevada.

Sam retrieved a bundle of letters from the truck cab and tossed them to Ander, then joined Zach at the corral. "So, what do you think?"

121

"This is great! Really." Zach pointed to the horses. "Benat doesn't use a truck or four-wheeler?"

"No. He believes in herding sheep the old-fashioned way. I don't even think Benat has a driver's license."

"How does he get into town if he needs something?"

"He rides down to the highway and uses a phone booth to call the Nevada. One of us brings up what he needs or picks him up and drives him into town. He doesn't call very often. Aside from food, most everything he needs is up in these hills. Except for his granddaughter, of course."

Catalin led Benat over to the corral by the hand and introduced Zach. Benat crunched Zach's hand and gave him a bright smile. "You are welcome at my sheep camp!"

Catalin's grandfather looked like a bear. He had a barrel chest, broad shoulders, and alert eyes the color of black diamonds. His complexion was dark, cured by years of sun and high desert wind.

Benat looked at Sam. "I need to check on the sheep before dark. Ander will be worthless until after he's read his letters from his sweetheart. Do you want to go for a ride, Unai?"

Instead of answering, Sam untied a set of reins and swung into the saddle easily. "What are we waiting for?"

"Why does he call Sam, Unai?" Zach asked.

"It's just a nickname he has for him," Catalin explained. "In Basque it means shepherd. My grandfather says that in his heart Sam is a Basque shepherd. But instead of sheep, his flock are the schoolchildren. He watches over us."

Zach had certainly experienced that. Benat shouted something at Ander, mounted his horse, and they trotted away.

"What did he say?" Zach asked.

"He told Ander that if dinner wasn't ready by the time they got back, there would be no more wine for a week," Catalin said. "He doesn't mean it, and Ander knows it. Want to go for a walk?"

They walked to the top of a small rise above camp to a rock outcrop, and looked across to the hillside where Benat and Sam rode along the edges of the vast sheep herd.

"What are they looking for?" Zach asked.

"Sick or injured sheep. Strays. Coyote signs. Anything unusual." Catalin started down the other side of the rise. "There's a canyon down here. It's my favorite place in the mountains."

Zach followed her.

"I guess this is quite a bit different from Oregon," she said.

Zach felt uneasy. "Yeah. I'm used to a lot more trees."

At the bottom of the canyon they came to a game trail and followed it in the waning sunlight. The air had a spicy smell to it that Zach had not encountered before.

"Do you miss Oregon?"

"I don't know." His discomfort grew. "I don't think about it much."

"How about your friends? You must miss them."

Zach wished she would change the subject. "I miss them sometimes." Which was true. "But I've made a lot of new friends here." Which was a little exaggeration.

"Did you have a girlfriend in Oregon?"

Zach turned red.

"I'm sorry," Catalin said quickly. "I guess that's none of my business."

"No, that's okay." Zach hesitated. "I didn't have a girl-friend." Although there had been a girl at his old school he had been interested in.

"Your mom's opening a bookstore?"

Zach nodded.

"So, what does your dad do?"

Dad? Zach thought. Oh, he's an international drug smuggler. "I'm not sure. I haven't seen him in a while." Zach took the initiative and changed the subject himself. "I've noticed you and your friends reading books in the cafeteria."

"I guess you started a fad," Catalin said.

Zach laughed. A rabbit flushed ahead of them. "Thanks for inviting me up here."

She smiled. "We better get back before my grandfather starts to worry about us."

"I guess we should," Zach said.

Catalin took his hand and they walked back up the trail. When they reached camp, Ander had dinner well underway on the stove inside the tent, Benat was tending the horses, and Sam was building a campfire.

"I'll help Ander with dinner," Catalin said. "Not that he needs it." She went into the tent.

Zach helped Sam with the fire, wondering if he now had a girlfriend. By the time they had the fire going, dinner was ready. Catalin came out of the tent and sat next to Zach. A moment later Ander came out carrying two loaves of freshly baked bread and a wheel of cheese. "The meat will be done soon," he said. They sat around the fire tearing off pieces of bread and slicing thick slabs of cheese from the wheel with Ander's hunting knife.

"How is your mother?" Benat asked Catalin.

"She's mad at you."

"She is always mad at me."

"She says that if you don't come down to the hotel in the next two weeks she is sending people up to bring you down."

"Ha! She said that?"

"She means it!"

"We will see."

"You've had fair warning, Grandpa."

"That's all a man can ask for." Benat sniffed the air. "Thank God you brought us steaks. We have been eating nothing but mutton for the past ten days."

Ander went into the tent and came back out with a plate piled with steaks and a pot of boiled potatoes. It was hard for Zach to believe that anything could taste better than the meal he had eaten at the hotel the night before, but it did. He was beginning to understand why Benat stayed up in the mountains.

After they ate, the men passed around a leather bag of red wine and squirted the juice into their mouths with their heads thrown back. Sam was as skilled with the bag as Benat and Ander.

"I think when I grow up I want to be a sheep herder," Zach told Catalin.

"There are worse things to be," she said. "But you're a little late. Most sheep these days are raised on huge corporate ranches in the flatlands. They feed the sheep medicated pellets and high-nutrient hay so they grow faster. And before you decide to become a shepherd you need to try herding during the winter when it's really cold. I don't know how they can stand it."

"Who owns these sheep?"

"Benat. And he loses money every year, according to my mother. The hotel and restaurant make up for what he loses out here. He pays Ander well and makes him put half his money in a special account that he can't touch until his contract is up. Ander has been here for two years. He has another year to go."

"Will he go back?"

"Hard to say. He has a girlfriend back home. He'll either go back to her or he'll try to save enough money to have her come over here."

Ander went into the tent and came back out with an old, battered guitar and a small accordion. He gave the guitar to Benat and they began to play and sing.

Zach did not understand the words, but it didn't matter.

14

Monday, October 2

I woke up before dawn and stayed in my sleeping bag stargazing until the sun took them away. I slipped out of my bag quietly and walked up to the rise above camp. It's cold! Frost on the grass. I can hear the sheep. A thin wisp of smoke is coming out of the tent's stovepipe where Catalin, Benat, and Ander are sleeping. Sam is curled up in his bag like a cocoon next to the campfire. I'm glad I brought my journal. I have a lot to write about.

A week ago, I had no friends. This morning I'm up in the Ruby Mountains with a girl that I can't seem to stop thinking about—a girl who doesn't even know my real name or the color of my eyes and probably never will. Uncle Don and Aunt Doris didn't prepare me for this.

Sam is up. He looks up here and waves. I wave back. He begins to put wood on the fire. I should go down and help him. What about Sam? He seems to have worked his way into our lives, or maybe we've worked our way into his. He is a composer, he speaks Basque, reads Russian—not your everyday custodian.

Ander comes out of the tent and helps Sam with the fire. And there's Catalin, stretching her arms above her head before putting on her down vest. She sees my empty sleeping bag and looks around. Sam says something to her and she looks to the top of the rise. And now she's coming my way. I like the way she moves. I like everything about this girl. I just wish I could tell her who I really am, but . . .

Zach closed the journal.

"So that's what you keep in the backpack," Catalin said.

He put the journal away.

"You're a writer as well as a reader."

"Not really," Zach said. "It's just my way of keeping track of things."

Catalin sat down next to him. "You sleep well?"

"Yeah. The Rubies are great. I hate to leave."

"So, Zachary Granger, tell me more about your mom and sister."

"Like what?"

"What are they like."

"Like twins," he said.

"What do you mean?"

"Same color hair, same eyes, same height. You'd know they were related if you saw them. Wanda is a senior in high school. She wants to be an actress. She's trying out for the lead in Sam's opera."

"What about your mom?"

"She's opening a bookstore."

"That's it?"

"Pretty much."

"And what about Zach Granger?"

Zach smiled. "He wants to grow up to be a sheep herder. Pretty simple."

"I have a feeling that there's nothing simple about Zachary Granger," Catalin said. "I think there's a lot more to him that he isn't saying."

Zach stood. How could he get to know someone if he couldn't talk about himself? "Smells like they're cooking breakfast down there."

"You're changing the subject."

"I'm hungry."

"We brought them fresh eggs. Not a lot of chickens up here. Ander nearly cried when he saw them."

"Think he'll share them?" Zach smiled.

"The Basques are very generous people."

15

Friday, October 6

*Commander IF is back. I was putting a book in my backpack and
he fell out on the bed. His head is back on his neck. He told me
Catalin slipped him into the backpack when we were up in the
Rubies. She knew he was my friend all along, but she didn't want
to embarrass me by pushing the issue. What a girl. Commander IF
misses her.*

*Catalin and I have started walking to school together. We
might as well, because Everyone knows Everything about
Everybody. On Tuesday half a dozen different people came up and
asked me if I enjoyed Benat's sheep camp. Translation: What's
going on between you and Catalin? I told them I had a great time.
Even Wanda knows about Catalin and me. She said that a sister of
someone who goes to my school told her. She didn't tease me about*

it, which makes me think that this maturity role she's playing isn't all bad. Everyone seems happy about me and Catalin except for Peter Short. He was waiting for me at my locker after school yesterday. His eye is kind of an ugly yellow now. He told me to stay away from Catalin. I told him to forget it. I'm sure I haven't heard the last of this from Peter, but I'm not worried about him.

A secretary came into Zach's homeroom and handed Ms. Miller a note.

"Darrell Gill and Zach Granger," Ms. Miller said. "You are both to go to Mr. Sebesta's room."

Zach and Darrell looked at each other from across the room.

"Now?" Darrell asked.

"Now," Ms. Miller said.

Out in the hallway, Zach asked Darrell what he had done.

"I was going to ask you the same thing," Darrell said.

When they got to Sam's room they found him pushing a hydraulic lift on wheels underneath one of the trapdoors in the ceiling.

"Thanks for coming," Sam said.

"Like we had a choice," Darrell scoffed. "What did we do wrong?"

"Not a thing. I wanted to make you boys a proposition." He locked the wheels on the lift and walked over to them. "You know we're doing this stage production of *The Opera Ghost*. I need a couple more stagehands. I thought you might be interested."

Darrell eyed Sam suspiciously. "What would we have to do?"

"Mostly grunt work. I'll have several high school kids helping as well, but it might be handy to have a couple people here at the school in case I need some help during the day."

Darrell smiled. "You mean we would have to miss class sometimes?"

"Not very often, but as we get closer to production day . . ."

"I'm in!" Darrell said quickly.

"I thought you might be. There will be some weekend and evening work too. How about you, Zach?"

"What about your building?"

"I'm not in any hurry to get it finished. It's been a mess for longer than I've been in Elko."

Because of Catalin, Zach wasn't in a hurry to get it done either, but becoming a stagehand meant he would be spending less time next door to the Nevada and he wasn't thrilled about that prospect.

Sam saw his hesitation. "I'll tell you what I'll do. I can't pay you anything, but if you have to work here weekends I'll treat you both to dinner at the hotel."

"In that case," Zach said, "I'm in, too."

"Good. Do you have time for a short tour?"

Darrell glanced at the clock. "We have time for a long tour."

Sam started by showing them the trapdoors. "They're hazards, and I should have nailed them shut long ago, but I'm glad I didn't, because we're going to use them in a couple of scenes. There are ten of them and they're controlled by these levers." He led them over to the workbench. "The levers are numbered and each lever has its own padlock. The padlocks are marked with corresponding numbers in red, and I have the only keys. If a padlock is hanging on the hook above the lever, that means the lever is hot. Which means don't touch it."

"Kind of a long fall," Darrell said, looking up at one of the trapdoors.

"That's why I have this lift. We put it under the trapdoor we're using. It works like an elevator. There's not much else to explain down here. I guess we can move up to the stage where most of the work will be done."

As Zach and Darrell passed the punching bag hanging beneath door number eight, they both took a swing at it. When they got up to the stage, Sam demonstrated how the lights were operated.

"Now, you probably won't be operating the lights. I'll have a crew from the high school do that."

"So what will we be doing?" Darrell asked.

"You'll be moving props around in between acts and helping to raise and lower backdrops. I'll show you." They followed him over to a series of ropes tied to cleats in the wall. "It's all done with block and tackle on a pulley system."

Zach and Darrell prolonged the tour as long as they could.

El Sereno was going through June Saunders's mail, envelope by envelope. When he came across a personal letter he set it in a separate pile to be opened and read later. He was almost at the bottom of the stack when he came to a postcard with a photo of the space shuttle on it. The only writing on the other side was June Saunders's address. He looked at the postmark on the card and smiled. The Osbornes were in Elko, Nevada. Or at least they had been on September twenty-ninth. He called Alonzo.

"We will go to Elko," Alonzo said. "What will you do with the postcard?"

El Sereno tore the postcard into small pieces and dropped them into the waste can. "I'm afraid it got lost in the mail."

Alonzo got on the intercom and told the pilot to change his course to Elko, Nevada. Paul and Berry were aboard.

Saturday, October 7

I'm at Sam's building. Catalin just brought lunch over to me and said she would be right back, so I thought I'd take a few minutes to write some things down. . . .

Journal #5 is just about used up, and it's my last one. I doubt I'll be able to find another one like it here in Elko. Maybe Mom can find something similar in one of the retail catalogs she's constantly poring over.

I've gotten most of the sawdust out of the building. This morning Sam supplied me with paint, drop cloths, brushes, and rollers. Then he went over to the bookstore. I haven't been there since they started, but Mom says the shelves are up and it's beginning to look like a bookstore.

Someone from the hotel left for the mountains this morning to pick up Benat. He had sent word that he would come down for a week under the condition that Sam, Catalin, and I take him back up and spend at least another night in the mountains with him. I'm looking forward to it.

So, the "Grangers" have settled into their new lives. Ten days ago I would not have believed this was possible. The only thing we're missing is Dad. Last night I asked Mom how she thought he was doing. She said she hoped he was okay. I asked her if she thought they would let him out. She said that even though he's cooperating with the DEA there was a good chance that he was going to serve some time, but the most important thing was that he is safe where he is.

I asked her what would happen after he got out. Would he join us here in Elko? She said she didn't know and went into her bedroom.

Dad really screwed things up for us, but I sure miss him. . . .

Catalin came back into the building. Zach wiped the tears away with his shirtsleeve and put the journal into his backpack.

"Is everything all right, Zach?"

He looked away. "Yeah. No problem."

She sat down next to him. "I've been meaning to talk to you about something," she said.

"Go ahead."

"When we were up in the mountains I asked you about your family and what it was like in Portland. I was trying to learn something about you, but every time I brought the subject up you changed it."

Zach didn't want to lie to Catalin, but couldn't tell her the truth. "Look," he said. "We had some very rough times where we used to live and I'm trying to forget them. If it's all the same to you I would like to leave the past where it belongs and get on with my life here in Elko. I hope that's okay."

"I like you, Zach, and I want to know you better."

"I like you, too." He took her hand. "Someday maybe I'll tell you about it, but for now let's just leave it alone."

"Okay."

"Besides," Zach added. "Curiosity killed the cat."

"Very funny, and not too original, either." She punched him in the arm.

"What can you expect from a guy who's been breathing sawdust for a week?" Zach jumped off the bench. "Speaking of which, I better get back to work."

"I'll give you a hand for a while. I don't have to start in the kitchen for another hour or so."

He handed her a roller. "Sam wants everything white, including the ceiling."

They worked steadily over the next hour in contented silence. When the wall was finished they stepped back to take a look at their work.

"It's going to need several more coats," Zach said. "But it does brighten up the room."

"After you're finished painting what do you think Sam will have you do next?"

"I don't know. The painting is going to take a long time."

"Maybe I shouldn't be helping you," Catalin said with mock seriousness. "By helping I'm taking food out of your mouth. I bet I've taken half a dinner away by just the little I've done today."

Zach laughed. "I hadn't thought of that. I guess you should put that roller down."

"What are you two doing in here?" someone behind them asked.

"Benat!" Catalin ran to the open door and threw her arms around him. "Does Mama know you're here?"

"No. They dropped me off and I saw light coming from this old building. I became suspicious."

"Of what?"

"Changes." He looked at Zach. "You are coming up to the camp next weekend?"

"Yes sir."

"I hope Unai is paying you well. This looks like very miserable work to me."

"He is. And I get free dinners at your restaurant."

"And good company," Benat said in Basque, looking at his granddaughter.

Catalin turned red.

"What did he say?"

"Nothing important."

Once or twice a week, Peter Short's parents left him a note to meet them someplace for dinner. These were about the only times he saw them, because they spent their nights gambling and slept most of the day. He was in no hurry. His parents were usually late, and sometimes if the cards were running well, they didn't show up at all.

He walked slowly by the Nevada Hotel hoping to run into Catalin. He did this often and was rarely rewarded.

If I had my own money, he thought, I'd eat dinner at the

Nevada every night Catalin was working. If I had *a lot* of money, I would get out of Elko and join my brother in San Francisco.

Peter's brother, Ted, was ten years older. He hadn't seen Ted since he was four years old. In fact he hadn't heard from Ted in all the years he had been in Elko. Then last summer, out of the blue, Ted had written and invited him to visit if he was ever in San Francisco. Peter asked his parents for the bus fare, but something always came up.

If his parents showed, maybe he could talk them into taking him to the Nevada for dinner instead of the cheap casino buffets they usually picked.

He saw a light in the building next to the Nevada and walked over to it. He had heard about Sam hiring Zach Granger to clean it. He tried the door. It wasn't locked. He put his head inside and saw the freshly painted wall. No sign of Zach, but sitting on a table on the far side was the leather backpack Zach was always carrying around. Peter stepped into the building.

Part Three

ZACH IN THE BOX

"Zach, you are going to Los Angeles with us tomorrow," his mother said.

It was early Thursday morning and Zach was in the kitchen eating a bowl of cereal, waiting for Wanda to get out of the bathroom. If she didn't come out in the next few minutes, Catalin would have to walk to school without him. In their former house they had had three and a half bathrooms.

"I really don't want to go, Mom," he said. "I have a lot of things going on at school. I'm a stagehand now, you know. I'm supposed to stay after school Friday and help Sam."

"I'm sure he can spare you for one day. I'm sorry I didn't give you more warning, but I just found out about the book convention yesterday. Publishers from all over the country will be there as well as retailers. It will give me a chance to meet them and get some tips for my bookstore. A lot of famous authors will be speaking and signing books.

You'll have a good time. While we're there we'll take Wanda over to the UCLA campus for a quick tour."

"Catalin's grandfather is in town and I was going to ride up to the Rubies on Saturday when they take him back. I really don't want to miss that."

"I'm sure you don't," his mother said. "Now, on a completely different subject. I was talking to a salesman at the bookstore yesterday and he said something about you getting into a fight with a boy at school."

Zach nearly dropped his spoon. *Everyone* knows *Everything* about *Everybody*. He would have to tell Darrell there was a fourth E in Elko. "*Eventually*," Zach mumbled.

"What did you say?"

"I wouldn't call it a fight," Zach said. "It was more like a little scuffle. It happened weeks ago. No big deal."

"It is a big deal, and I don't want you fighting or scuffling," she told him. "And you're coming with us to Los Angeles. I can't leave you in the house alone."

"Why not? I stayed in our old house alone, and you didn't have a problem with it back then."

"It's different now."

"Yeah, I'm older," Zach said.

"You know what I mean."

Zach knew, but it still seemed ridiculous. "How about if I stayed with Sam?"

"I couldn't ask him to do that."

"You don't have to," Zach said. "I will."

"It's too much of an imposition. He's an old man with friends and a life of his own. He doesn't need a boy underfoot."

"Just let me ask him," Zach pleaded. "If he says no then I'll go with you without complaint."

His mother thought about it for a moment. "Let's take it a step further than that," she said. "If you ask him and he says yes, tell him to come by the store after school, and I'll be the judge of his enthusiasm and let you know."

"It's a deal."

Wanda came out of the bathroom with a towel wrapped around her head like a turban. "I'm not finished in there," she said.

"I'll only be a minute." Zach dashed for the bathroom and slammed the door.

"I mean it, Zach!" Wanda shouted at the door. "This is an important day for me. The *Opera Ghost* auditions are today."

Mrs. Osborne looked at her watch. "Don't worry. If he's not out in two minutes, he won't be able to walk to school with his new friend."

Wanda laughed. "Oh, he'll be out, then."

Zach and Catalin got to school about ten minutes before the bell rang.

"I'm going to talk to Sam," Zach said. "I'll see you in homeroom."

He found Sam on top of the hydraulic lift trying to unhook the chain holding up the punching bag.

"Just in time," Sam said.

"What are you doing?" Zach asked.

"Clearing out a space so we'll have more room to work on the stage sets and props." He lowered the lift. "Let's switch places. I'll hold the bag up while you unhook the chain."

Zach got onto the lift and held the up button until he reached the ceiling.

"Ready?" Sam asked.

"Okay."

Sam wrapped his arms around the heavy bag and with a grunt lifted it up. Zach unsnapped the chain from the eye-bolt, and Sam dropped the bag with a thud.

"What are you going to do if someone needs the bag?" Zach asked, lowering the lift.

"I guess everyone will just have to stay out of trouble until the production is over. Why don't you and Darrell come back down here after school and we'll haul this bag out of here."

"What about the auditions?" The day before, Mrs. Pyle had made an announcement over the school intercom that students could not be anywhere near the auditorium during auditions.

"Oh, that's right. Maybe you and Darrell can come by after lunch and give me a hand."

"Sure. Where are we going to put it?

"We'll put it up on the stage. I'll get someone to haul it away later this week. What brought you down here, Zach?"

Zach explained the reason for his early-morning visit.

"You're more than welcome to stay with me at the Nevada," Sam said enthusiastically. "In fact, there's a spare room right now, and I'm sure Mrs. Cristobal wouldn't mind you bunking there for a couple days."

"Mom said that you're going to have to convince her that you really want me. She wanted to know if you could stop by the store this afternoon."

146

"I can't this afternoon," Sam said. "I expect the auditions to run late."

"You're sitting in on the auditions?"

"I'm on the high-school theater committee, and of course it's my opera."

"My sister's trying out for the part of Christine."

"I know," Sam said. "And from what I understand she has a good chance of getting the part. The high school drama instructor told me she has a voice like an angel. Wanda will have some competition though."

The bell rang. "I better go," Zach said. "If I'm late for PE, Mr. Dugan will make me run extra laps and climb the rope to the ceiling of the gym."

"Well, don't worry about this weekend. I'll drive over to the bookstore later this morning and square it with your mother."

Zach was late for PE and Mr. Dugan was in a foul mood. He made Zach climb the rope three times. He thought Mr. Dugan might skip the extra laps, but he didn't.

Still sweating after his shower, Zach willed his numb legs down the hallway to his homeroom, but his discomfort did not diminish his contentment. Before he sat down he stopped at Catalin's desk and told her the good news about staying at the Nevada. She was happy too. Zach sat down and began going through his binder trying to find the homework he had finished the night before, when he heard someone say, "Who's Commander IF?"

Zach's head snapped up. Written in big red letters on the chalkboard was:

Commander IF was here!

"I have no idea," Ms. Miller said. "But if I find out who wrote this they'll be spending time after school scrubbing my chalkboard, because this red chalk is nearly impossible to erase."

Zach stared in disbelief at the board. Catalin glanced back at him, smiling along with all the other students.

"This is not a good way to start the day," Ms. Miller continued. "Your homework had better be finished. Pranks like this put me in a very unforgiving mood."

Zach barely heard her. He looked around the room expecting to see at least one of his classmates smirking at him, but there were no smirks. Most of them were desperately trying to finish their homework, while others were stacking their assignments neatly on their desks for Ms. Miller to pick up. He quickly ran through all the possibilities.

First possibility: Pure coincidence—someone else had an imaginary friend. If his father and grandfather called their imaginary friend IF, there was a chance that the name was common. But what were the chances of someone naming their imaginary friend "Commander." Just about zero, Zach concluded.

Second possibility: his father was out of jail and was trying to get in touch with him. Not likely, Zach thought. His father would be a lot more direct. And as far as he knew, his father didn't even know they were living in Elko. Or their new last names for that matter.

Third possibility: his sister had told one of her friends about her weird brother and his imaginary friend. In turn they passed the information to their little brother or sister, who couldn't resist playing a joke on the new guy in school.

Elko's three E's again. This was the only reasonable explanation. He was going to kill Wanda.

The effect of the prank on the class seemed to be fading fast as Ms. Miller did her best to erase the sentence. By the time class ended everyone seemed to have forgotten about it, including Catalin, who didn't mention it once during lunch. She spent almost the whole lunch period talking about what they would do up in the Rubies.

Zach didn't hear half of what she said. He was still shaken by the chalkboard incident. A prank wasn't fun unless you confronted the victim, but no one had stepped forward yet, and this had him worried. He and Darrell left the cafeteria early to help Sam lug the punching bag up to the stage.

Peter Short watched Zach and Darrell get up and leave the cafeteria. He wondered what Zach's reaction would have been if he had joined them at the table with the *book* he was reading at home. The thought brought a smile to his face.

"What's so funny, Peter?" his lunch partner asked.

"Nothing," Peter said quickly, getting rid of the smile. He would have to be careful or his fun would be over before it really got going. One of the things his father had taught him was to play his cards close to his chest. *Never show them what you have. Keep a poker face. Something as small as a twitch of an eye can give your hand away and the game is over. Be patient.* Peter was enjoying this game too much for it to be over. He had told no one about what he had found. He had resisted the temptation to write on the board until this morning. He had been patient.

* * *

The final bell rang, and still no one had approached Zach about Commander IF. He concluded that Ms. Miller's negative reaction must have scared them off.

After school, Darrell was waiting for him at his locker. "Want to see the *Phantom* auditions?"

"It's a closed audition," Zach said. "The only people allowed into the auditorium are the people trying out and the teachers involved in the production."

Darrell smiled. "They'll all be sitting down below. I was upstairs earlier today, and you know what I discovered?"

Zach shook his head.

"One of the balcony doors is unlocked. It's dark up there and if we sit toward the back, no one will see us."

Catalin's mother had picked her up early from school for a dentist appointment. The only thing Zach had to do after school was talk to his sister, but he wouldn't be able to do that until she got home from the auditions.

"Who else knows about the door?" Zach wasn't about to sneak up there with a crowd of kids. As soon as a nervous high school student hit a wrong note, one of them would start laughing and they would get caught.

"Just the two trusty stagehands," Darrell said. "In fact, Sam probably would have let us sit in on the audition if we had asked."

Zach seriously doubted that. But he did want to see Wanda audition. He put his things in his locker and they went upstairs to find their seats.

18

Peter Short waited in the park across the street from Elko Middle School. Soon, most everyone in the building would be in the auditorium watching the auditions, which meant Peter could slip in and out of Ms. Miller's room without being seen playing his second card. He gave it five more minutes, then started across the street, but he did not get very far.

"Excuse me," a voice called from behind him.

Peter turned around and saw a man dressed entirely in black.

"Do you go to this school?" the man asked.

"Why do you want to know?"

The man smiled easily with the whitest set of teeth Peter had ever seen. He had black hair, pulled back into a short ponytail. He wore a black leather coat over a black shirt, tight black jeans, and black cowboy boots with gold tips on the toes. Peter could not believe his bad luck.

"My name is Hector Jones," the man said.

"Good to meet you, Hector. What do you want? I'm in kind of a hurry."

"And your name is?"

"Peter Short."

Hector put his hand out. On his wrist was a heavy gold watch. On three of his fingers were expensive-looking rings. Peter became a lot more interested in Hector Jones. He shook Hector's hand.

"Have you gone to this school long, Peter?"

"Since sixth grade. I'm in eighth now." Who was this guy? What did he want?

Hector looked up and down the street. "A lot of cars."

"They're having auditions for the high school play today," Peter explained.

Hector looked closely at Peter's face. "That must have been quite a black eye at one time."

"You should have seen the other guy," Peter said.

Hector gave a small laugh. "I'm wondering if I can trust you, Peter."

Peter didn't say anything.

"I am in town looking for someone, but it is very important that they do not know that I am looking for them. Do you understand?"

"Yeah, I understand."

Hector reached into his pocket and came out with a thick roll of bills. He peeled off two twenties. "If I ask you some questions, can you keep it just between you and me?"

Peter stared at the money. "I can keep my mouth shut."

"I thought you could." He handed Peter the bills. "Do

you get a lot of new students here?"

"Quite a few."

"The family I'm looking for has a son about your age. Brown hair, brown eyes, a little taller than you. Anyone like that around here?"

Peter thought immediately of Zach Granger, but he had blue eyes. There were a couple other new kids in school it could be, too. "What's their last name?"

"They used to go by the name Osborne, but I suspect they are no longer using that name."

"Why are you looking for them?"

"Mrs. Osborne left her husband. He wants to know where his children are. He wants to know if they are safe."

"Are you a private detective or something?"

"Yes."

"Is there a reward?"

"Two hundred dollars."

Might be enough to get to San Francisco, Peter thought. "Do you have a photo of the family?"

"I am afraid I don't," Hector said. "Do you think you know a boy like this?"

Never show them what you have. Peter wasn't sure if he had anything or not, but he wasn't going to tell Hector this. "Like I said, there are a lot of new kids this year. It's possible that one of them could be who you're looking for. I could do some asking around. How do I get in touch with you?"

"I'm staying at the Windsor Hotel. Room 222."

"What are you going to do when you find them?"

"I will tell Mr. Osborne where they are. It will be up to the courts to decide what to do next."

"I'll keep my eyes open."

"Thank you, Peter. I'm glad we met."

So was Peter. He decided to go home and take another look at Zach's journal. He had only skimmed it before, looking for references to Catalin. Tonight he would read it all the way through. His second card could wait.

Zach and Darrell sat in the back row of the balcony listening to nervous high school students audition for the part of Eric, the opera ghost. It was down to two boys. One had a very good singing voice, but he was short and a little overweight—not Zach's idea for this character. The other finalist was a tall, muscular, good-looking kid who couldn't hold a tune.

Sam was standing to the side of the stage talking with a group of adults. After a brief conference, Sam walked over to the short boy and shook his hand. There was a subdued applause.

"That guy is going to play the lead?" Darrell asked.

"It's an opera, Darrell. The lead has to be able to sing. It's not like the movies where they hire the best-looking guy they can find regardless of acting talent. In opera looks aren't that important."

"Maybe you should take voice lessons," Darrell said.

"Maybe you should shut up."

Wanda and another girl came onto the stage.

"I guess they're going to cast the part of Christine next," Zach said.

"Which one's your sister?"

"The blonde with the short hair."

"Wow!"

"Didn't I tell you to shut up?"

The people below took their seats and the first girl moved to her position on center stage. A minute later The Phantom walked onto the stage and stood next to her.

"Who's in the Phantom costume?" Darrell asked.

"Sam." Zach recognized the khaki pants beneath the black cape.

The girl began to sing to The Phantom.

"She's pretty good," Darrell whispered.

Zach nodded. The girl was surprisingly good. At their old school, Wanda didn't have much in the way of competition. Midway through the girl's song, the balcony door opened.

"Get down!" Darrell hissed.

They ducked below the seatbacks and peered at the intruder through the gaps. He was dressed in black. In the dim light Zach could not make out his features, but the ponytail was clear enough. The man glanced around the balcony for a moment then found a seat four rows down from where they were hiding. Unfortunately, the man was now between them and the door. Zach looked at Darrell and rolled his eyes, wondering who the man was, why he was there, and most importantly, how long they would be trapped.

The first Christine finished her song to loud applause. Crouched behind the seat, Zach and Darrell could not see the stage. After a while things quieted down and the music started again.

Wanda's voice literally filled the auditorium from her very first note. The man with the ponytail leaned forward in his seat.

"Wow," Darrell whispered.

Zach nodded in agreement. He had heard Wanda sing the song a dozen times around the house, but it hadn't sounded anything like this. If he didn't know better, he would swear there was a Broadway star singing on stage.

The man in black got up and left the balcony before Wanda finished the song. Zach and Darrell got back into their seats just in time to see Wanda hit her last note. Zach had never been more proud of his sister.

When the song ended there was no applause—at first. Wanda stood on the stage with her head bowed, almost as if she were praying. Zach wondered what she was thinking about at that moment. The Phantom stood a few feet away just looking at her as if he couldn't believe what he had just heard. Someone began clapping and was joined by others. Then everyone got up and gave Wanda a standing ovation.

In his excitement over his sister's performance, Zach forgot about the man in black until he and Darrell were standing in front of his house.

"What do you think that guy was doing in the balcony?"

"Never seen him before," Darrell said. "Probably a parent, though. Snuck in for a look like we did. I guess we didn't have to hide. If he'd told on us he would get busted, too. They don't allow parents into auditions."

"He left before Wanda finished." Which seemed very odd to Zach.

"He was probably the first girl's father," Darrell said. "As soon as he heard your sister he knew it was all over for his daughter. See you tomorrow." Darrell continued down the block to his house.

Zach's mother was in her bedroom packing for her trip.

"I've got good news," she said. "Mr. Sebesta would be delighted to have you as his weekend guest."

Sam had already told him. "Thanks for letting me stay, Mom."

"And," she continued, "I asked him about this so-called scuffle you had at school."

Uh-oh, Zach thought.

"Seems that the other boy got a black eye out of the deal. Mr. Sebesta said it wasn't your fault, but—"

At that moment, Wanda burst into the house announcing that she had gotten the part of Christine. "I flubbed the song a little, but they gave it to me anyway."

Wanda hadn't flubbed a note as far as Zach could tell, but he couldn't say anything because he wasn't supposed to have been there.

"That's wonderful!" Zach's mom said. "I'm so proud of you." She gave Wanda a hug.

Zach wanted to talk to Wanda about Commander IF, but he wasn't able to get her alone. She spent the whole evening with their mother packing and talking about the play, the bookstore, and what they would do in Los Angeles. Zach finally gave up and went to bed, hoping to catch her alone before they went to the airport.

Around two in the morning Zach was awakened by a light

tapping on his door.

He turned the light on. "Yeah?"

Wanda came into his room, closing the door quietly behind her, and sat on the edge of the bed. It looked like she had been crying.

"What's the matter?"

"I can't sleep," she said. "I've been thinking about Dad."

"Oh."

"It really hit me today during the audition. To bring the right emotion to the song I tried to think of the saddest thing I could. I thought about how Dad used to be, and what's happening to him now. Oh, Jack!" She threw her arms around him and started to cry. He held her, and for a moment, they were Jack and Joanne Osborne again.

19

"Here's the number of our hotel," Zach's mother said. "Are you sure you'll be all right?"

"Yes, Mom."

"We'll be home early Sunday evening. Do you know when you'll be down from the mountains?"

"Late, probably."

"Not too late. You have school on Monday."

"I gotta go."

Zach kissed his mother and was tempted to kiss his sister as well. He felt a lot closer to her than he had in a long time. He hadn't talked to her about Commander IF. It would have to wait until she got back from Los Angeles. He gave her a big smile and said, "Don't let some Hollywood producer lure you away."

"Not much chance."

Zach wasn't so sure, after hearing her performance.

He got to Catalin's house just as she was stepping out her front door.

"Zach, I understand you'll be staying with us at the Nevada tonight," Mrs. Cristobal said.

"I hope that's all right," Zach said.

"Of course it's all right. We enjoy your company."

The school day started out well. Mr. Dugan was home with the flu. The substitute thought PE meant Pretty Easy, and for the first time since Zach had started school, he walked into his homeroom sweat-free. This changed as soon as he took his seat. Scrawled across the chalkboard in very big, clumsy letters was:

If you take the "v" out of lives
what do you get?

"I don't think this is at all funny!" Ms. Miller said. "It took me a half an hour to get the red chalk off the board yesterday. I want to know who did this."

Zach stared straight ahead unable to believe what he was seeing. His sister had not told a friend about Commander IF. Someone had read about Commander IF in his journal.

"Well?" Ms. Miller asked.

No one answered.

"Fine." She stepped over to the intercom and called the principal.

It took Mrs. Pyle less than a minute to get to the room. She looked at the scrawled sentence for a long time, then turned to the class.

"Someone in here knows something about this," Mrs.

Pyle said and looked from student to student, lingering a little longer when she got to Zach, who was frantically trying to remember the last time he had seen his journal.

The leather backpack was hanging on the doorknob of his bedroom door. This he knew. He had seen it just that morning and had almost slipped the pack over his shoulder on his way out, but decided he would pick it up after school instead. But was the journal in the backpack? When was the last time he had seen the journal? Today was the 13th of October. Friday the 13th. That's just about perfect, he thought bitterly. He had made his last entry on Saturday while he was working in the building. He remembered that he was getting to the end of the journal and had decided to cut back on the entries until he found a replacement for it.

"Zach?"

If he had lost the journal, or someone had stolen it . . .

"Zachary?"

. . . his mother would have to give up her bookstore. His sister would lose her part in *The Opera Ghost*. He would lose Catalin. It seemed impossible that he had been the one who had slipped—

"Zachary Granger!"

A hand slammed down on his desk. The classroom came back into focus. Mrs. Pyle had somehow materialized in front of his desk and was looking down at him with a horrible scowl.

She pointed at the board. "What do you know about this, Zach?"

"Nothing," he said quietly.

"What?"

"I said I don't know anything about it!"

"What time did you arrive at school today?"

"Just before the bell. I didn't do this."

Catalin came to his defense. "He's right, Mrs. Pyle. Zach and I walked to school together this morning. We got here just before the bell rang."

Mrs. Pyle stared at Zach. "What did you do yesterday after school?"

"I was with Darrell."

Mrs. Pyle looked over at Darrell. "And what did you do after school?"

"We played video games at my house," Darrell said with perfectly straight face. "I annihilated him."

Several kids laughed. It occurred to Zach that Darrell was much better suited for the Witness Security Program than he was.

Mrs. Pyle addressed the entire class. "If it happens again, you will all stay after school and scrub every chalkboard in this building." Before she left the room she shot Zach another scowl.

Scrubbing chalkboards was the least of Zach's problems. He had to get home and find out if his journal was still in the backpack, but he would have to wait until lunch. He couldn't leave early without getting a pass from the office, which would mean another encounter with Mrs. Pyle. He glanced at the clock every three minutes thinking that at least half an hour had passed. When the bell finally rang it was all he could do not to sprint out of the room at a dead run. He followed the others through the door.

Catalin was waiting for him in the hallway. "Why do you think Mrs. Pyle thought you wrote on the board?"

"I don't know," Zach said.

"Are you okay? You looked kind of strange when Mrs. Pyle was talking to you."

"I just zoned out for a second or two."

Darrell walked up to them. "You two headed to lunch?"

"I've got to run home for a second," Zach answered.

"Why?" Catalin asked.

"I left my homework."

"Aren't you going to eat?"

"I'll get something at home," Zach said backing his way down the hallway. "I'll see you after lunch."

As soon as he got out of sight of the school he ran all the way home. He found his backpack hanging on the closet doorknob. He dumped the contents on the bed. Commander IF. Pencils. Erasers. Two books he was reading. No journal.

He sat on the edge of the bed and covered his face with his hands. He thought of his laundry hamper and jumped up. It wouldn't be the first time he had hidden the journal in there. He turned it over and shook it out. Socks. Underwear. Shirts. Pants. No journal.

Zach cursed.

The only other place it might be was in the Jack in the Box. There was a chance he might have put it in there and forgotten he had done it. He pulled the box down from the closet shelf without much hope and put it on the bed.

"Five journals," Zach said out loud. "That's all I ask. If there are five in the box I promise I'll never *slip up* again. In fact, I'll burn them and forget Jack Osborne ever existed."

Zach pulled the chain with the Jack in the Box key over his head. He opened the padlock, closed his eyes, lifted the lid, then turned the box upside down. He opened his eyes. There were five journals lying on the bed, but one of them wasn't his.

The fifth journal was scuffed and battered and had a rubber band around it to hold the pages in. He took the rubber band off and opened the cover. Paper-clipped to the first page was a note from his father.

Jacko,

I'm sorry I had to use your box. I didn't know where else to put this thing. I'm also sorry you found this before I was ready.

Whatever you do, don't read this journal! The information it contains will just get you in trouble. Above all else, keep the journal safe. I'll get in touch with you when I need it.

Love, Dad

Zach reread the note three times. The binding on the journal had come apart and all the pages inside were loose. On the first page was a sketch of a man's face. Beneath the sketch was a name: Alonzo Aznar. Under the name were Alonzo Aznar's vital statistics: age, height, weight, hair color, eye color, and various addresses.

Despite his father's warning, Zach flipped through a few more pages. On them were more sketches, locations of remote landing strips, addresses, and rows of accounting information, all in his father's neat handwriting. Zach slipped the rubber band back around the journal. He looked at the other journals lying on the bed. There was no point in burning them now. Number five was gone. Someone knew who they were. It was only a matter of time before the Grangers became someone else.

"What rhymes with Zach?" he asked.

Mack, Commander IF said.

Zach called the number of the hotel his mother had given him.

"I'm sorry," the receptionist said. "We don't have anyone here by the name of Granger."

"They probably haven't checked in yet," Zach said. "I'd like to leave a message. Have them call Zach as soon as they can."

He thought about hiding his father's journal, but he was afraid someone might find it. He decided to keep it with him until he could get it to his father.

20

Peter Short was disappointed when Zach didn't show up in the cafeteria for lunch. The school was buzzing with the news of the new chalkboard message and he wanted to see Zach's reaction to the second card he had played early that morning in Ms. Miller's room.

Peter's third card was going to be a bluff card. He had been up half the night studying the journal, but he still had some doubts about who Zach really was. He would have to play the third card in person. His chance came after lunch.

Zach was in no hurry to return to school. In fact he thought about skipping the afternoon altogether to wait by the phone for his mother to call back, but after a while sitting there by himself started to drive him crazy.

He was a half an hour late. He stopped in the office for a late slip, telling the secretary that going home had taken longer than he thought. She wrote out the slip, barely looking up at him. Zach was grateful that Mrs. Pyle's office door was closed. He stopped at his locker to get his math book, and decided to take another look at his dad's journal before going to class. As he pulled it out of the backpack, the rubber band snapped and the loose pages spilled all over the freshly waxed floor.

"Great!" He got down on his knees and hurriedly began gathering the pages.

"Did you drop these?"

Zach looked up. Peter Short was standing in front of him, holding a couple of loose pages. Zach stood up and grabbed them out of his hand. Peter laughed as Zach stuffed the pages into the tattered journal.

"Looks like you need a new journal, *Jack*," Peter said.

Zach began to feel queasy. "My name is Zach, not Jack."

Peter stopped smiling. Time for the third card. "Your name is Jack Osborne." And the fourth card. "Your sister's name is Joanne Osborne."

Zach closed his eyes in defeat. "How did you get my journal?"

Peter's smile returned. The bluff had worked. Until that moment he hadn't known for certain that Zach Granger was Jack Osborne. Zach had not written their old last name in the journal. The last name had come from the man looking for them—Hector Jones.

"What you should be asking me is what am I going to do with your journal."

"What are you going to do with it?"

"I haven't decided," Peter said. "That depends on you."

"Who have you told about it?"

"No one."

Zach felt a flicker of hope. "What do you want?"

Peter looked at the clock on the wall. "I need to get back to class. I'll meet you in the park at four o'clock and we can discuss it."

Zach stared at him. "How about if I go to Mrs. Pyle and tell her you have it?"

Peter laughed. "You're a terrible bluffer, Jack. If you tell her, I'll tell everyone in this school who you are." Peter walked away, then stopped and turned back for a second. "Does Catalin know your eyes aren't really blue?"

When Peter got to his class he unfolded the loose journal page he had stuffed into his pocket before Zach saw him standing there. The sketch on the torn page looked a lot like Hector Jones.

Zach knew he could not trust Peter. But if he could delay Peter long enough for his mother to get in touch with Uncle Don and Aunt Doris, the U.S. Marshals might have some way of keeping Peter's mouth shut. There was still hope.

After school Zach stopped by the custodian room.

"Your sister was amazing yesterday," Sam said. "She's going to make a great Christine."

Only if she changes her name to Christine in her next life, Zach thought. "Yeah, she's pretty excited."

"Did they make it to Los Angeles okay?"

"I haven't heard from them yet."

"What time are you coming over to the Nevada?

"I should be there by dinner."

Sam looked at Zach closely. "You know, you don't look

like a kid who's going up to the mountains with his girl-friend for the weekend. Is everything okay?"

"Sure."

"I heard about the note on the chalkboard. Mrs. Pyle was convinced that you were involved somehow."

"Well, she's wrong."

"I told her that it didn't seem like something you would do. Are you sure there's nothing going on you'd like to talk about?"

Zach shook his head and left the room.

When he got home the first thing he did was call his mother's hotel. They had still not checked in.

"I'd like to leave another message," Zach said.

"If they haven't checked in by now, they're not checking in," the woman said. "We're full. Are you sure this is the right hotel?"

"It's the only number she gave me."

"Well, there are no Grangers here and none on the reservation list. They must have gone to another hotel."

Zach hung the phone up and went into his mother's bedroom hoping to find the number for Uncle Don and Aunt Doris. It wasn't there. The only thing for him to do was to meet with Peter and see what he wanted. He packed a few things for his trip to the mountains and walked to the park across the street from the school.

Peter was looking at his watch. "You're late."

"Where's my journal?"

Peter reached into his backpack and pulled the journal out. "Here you go," he said cheerfully and handed it to him.

Zach was not expecting this.

"Don't look so shocked," Peter smirked. "I don't need your journal anymore. I already know what's in it."

The 3 E's. Peter knew how this worked better than most. All he had to do was tell the story to one person and the Grangers might as well change their name back to Osborne.

"What do you want?" Zach thought Peter would ask him for money, but he surprised him.

"I want you to break up with Cat," he said.

"Are you serious?"

"Dead serious."

"Why?"

"Call it a test."

"What am I supposed to say to her?"

"I don't care what you say to her. All I know is that it better work. If I hear of you walking to school with her, going up to the sheep camp, or anything else, everybody in town will know who you are."

When Zach got to the Nevada he went right in to the kitchen to find Catalin. She was mixing salad. Mrs. Cristobal intercepted him before he got to her.

"You will be in room nine," she said. "It's right next door to Sam's room. It has been empty for a while. I'm afraid there's not much in it, but it will only be for one night."

Two nights, Zach thought. He wasn't going up to the Rubies. "Thanks." He walked over to Catalin.

"Where were you after school?" she asked. "I looked all over for you."

"I went home to get my things."

"If it were up to Benat we would leave tonight, but my

mother wouldn't hear of it. We'll be leaving tomorrow early."

Zach looked around the crowded kitchen. He couldn't tell Catalin now. It would have to wait until after dinner. "I guess I'll go up and get settled in."

He went upstairs. The door to number nine was open, and Mrs. Cristobal was right, there was nothing in the room except a bed and a dresser.

Sam walked in behind him. "You all ready to go, Zach?"

"Yeah."

"Are you sure you're feeling okay?"

Sam had just given him his excuse for not going up to the Rubies. "I might be getting sick or something. Maybe the flu."

Sam looked concerned. "Maybe you should lie down for a while, see if you can shake it off."

"Good idea."

"Do you want to eat?"

"I don't know."

"Well, you just rest up for now. If you feel like eating later come on down."

"Thanks, Sam."

Zach put his backpack in the bottom drawer of the dresser and lay down on the bed.

Peter Short waited outside the Nugget Casino for his parents. There was a note in the trailer saying they wanted him to meet them for dinner. They were already a half an hour late. He was about ready to go home and make himself something to eat when his mother came out the door.

"Your father's a big winner tonight!" she said happily,

not mentioning a word about being forty-five minutes late.

"How much did he win?"

"Five thousand dollars!"

A moment later Peter's father came through the door flushed with excitement. "Hey, son. Want to go to Reno with us? Your mom and I want to take a run over there while the cards are working. We'll come back Sunday."

"I don't know," Peter said, trying not to show his disappointment. He knew from past experience that if his parents went to Reno they wouldn't leave until they had lost every cent they had won. "I have a lot of homework to do."

"No problem," his father said. Peter saw the relief in his father's face. He hadn't wanted Peter to go in the first place. "Guess you'll be on your own this weekend then. Wish my parents had trusted me like we trust you."

"Maybe you should leave enough money here for me to get that ticket to San Francisco," Peter said.

"What are you talking about?"

"You know, just in case you don't win in Reno."

"Are you trying to sabotage my luck or something? You know better than that. Don't worry about the trip to San Francisco. The cards are with us. When we get back, I'll buy you a first-class ticket to see your brother."

Peter knew better than to push it. "So, are you leaving now?"

"Not until after we eat," his mother said. "Where do you want to go?"

"Let's go to the Nevada," Peter said.

"Big spender," his father said. "No problem. We'll have the works."

21

Zach stayed up in his room until the smell of the Basque food drove him downstairs. He had not eaten since breakfast. He took a chair near Sam at the end of the long table.

"Feeling better," Sam asked.

"Not really, but thought I should eat something."

Benat Pasquale entertained the table with his stories. He had bought a round of drinks for everyone at the table except Zach, which had put everyone in a merry mood. Despite what he had to tell Catalin later, Zach felt his mood lighten a little under the influence of the men's laughter and good food.

Catalin brought in a huge bowl of salad and put it in front of Zach with a big smile. He couldn't help but smile back at her. How was he going to tell her that he did not want to see her again?

The Short family was shown to a table near the window.

As they came in Peter caught a glimpse of Cat going into the kitchen through the swinging door. He hoped she would wait on their table. She didn't. A minute later, she came back through the kitchen door balancing a platter of meat in each hand and headed for the long table with the Basque boarders. Peter followed her progress and was stunned when he saw Zach sitting at the end of the table with his back to him. Cat put the platters on the table, then stood next to Zach and said something to her grandfather. As she spoke, she rested her hand on Zach's shoulder. Peter was too far away to hear what she was saying, but whatever it was Zach must have found it amusing, because he laughed.

"You won't be laughing later, Jack," Peter muttered.

"What's that son?" his mother asked.

"Nothing." You called the wrong man's bluff, Peter thought. His parents began recounting their big win at the casino. He had heard it all before and tuned them out as he watched Cat come and go to the long table. On each trip she either said something to Zach or brushed up against him. By the time their food arrived, Peter was almost too angry to eat. His parents, on the other hand, gulped their food like starved wolves, eager to be on their way to Reno.

"So, what are you going to do while we're gone?" His father asked with a mouthful of mashed potatoes.

"Hang around the trailer, I guess."

"Well to be honest with you, there's a chance we won't be back by Sunday. Depends on how the cards are running."

"I'll be fine," Peter said. As if they cared. It didn't matter when they came back. He had already decided that he was

174

leaving Elko on the first available flight. He was going to play his last card, and by the time his parents came chugging back into town on empty, he would be in San Francisco. They probably wouldn't even notice he was gone.

"I'm going to take off," Peter said, standing up.

"We're done, too," his father said.

Catalin came into the dining room again and saw Peter and his parents walking out of the dining room. She walked over to the long table, took a hold of Zach's hand, and whispered something to him. Zach immediately pulled his hand out of hers and turned around. But Peter was no longer there. Zach ignored the look of shock on Catalin's face as he stood up, almost knocking his chair over.

"What's the matter, Zach?" Sam asked.

The table had gone quiet. The men stared at him.

"Nothing," Zach said. "I've got to go to the restroom." He didn't wait to see their response. He wove his way through the other tables hoping to catch Peter before he left, but he was too late. He stepped out the front door and saw two people getting into their car. He ran over to them.

"Excuse me," he said. "Aren't you Peter's parents?"

"We sure are," Peter's dad said.

"I'm a friend of his from school. I saw you in the Nevada eating. Where's Peter?"

"I think he went home," Peter's mother said. "He had a lot of homework to do."

"Oh," Zach said. "I was hoping to talk with him. I had a question about one of our assignments. Which direction did he go?"

"We have a place at the trailer park over on Cypress,"

Peter's dad said. "Number forty-two. If you hurry you can probably catch up to him before he gets there."

Zach ran all the way to the trailer park. When he got there he had a difficult time finding Peter's trailer in the dark. The numbers weren't marked very well. He didn't know exactly what he was going to say to Peter when he found him. He would apologize or something. Tell Peter that he hadn't had a chance to talk to Catalin alone. That he would have already broken up with her if Peter hadn't shown up at the Nevada.

He found the trailer. The lights were off. He knocked on the metal door, but no one answered. Now what? Zach sat down at the rickety picnic table in front of the trailer. Maybe Peter had stopped somewhere on his way home. He would have to show up eventually. Zach decided to wait for him.

Catalin knocked on Sam's door.

"Where's Zach?" she asked. "He's not in his room."

"I know," Sam said.

"What's going on?"

"I was going to ask you the same thing. Did anything happen today at school?"

"Zach's been acting strange all day, but he wouldn't talk about it. It started this morning when he saw writing on Ms. Miller's chalkboard."

"Well, I'm sure it's nothing to worry about. He must have gone home to get something." Catalin looked at him doubtfully.

"If he doesn't come back soon," Sam continued, "I'll get in the truck and see if I can find him."

"I'll go with you."

"No. You just go home with your folks. We need to get an early start tomorrow."

Catalin started to protest, but Sam put his hand up. "I'll have Zach give you a call when he gets back. It's nothing to worry about."

But Sam was very worried. He had just called Zach's house and no one had answered. He had known something was wrong when he saw Zach after school and was kicking himself for not pushing the issue more.

There was a knock on Alonzo Aznar's door. Paul got up and looked through the peephole.

"It's another kid."

"Let him in," Alonzo said. "Perhaps he has some news for us."

Paul opened the door and Peter stepped into the room.

Alonzo stared at the boy, trying to remember who he was. "I'm afraid I have forgotten your name."

"Peter."

"That's right. I believe I told you to call if you had information for me."

"I was going to," Peter said. "But I thought it would be better if I talked to you face-to-face."

"Please have a seat. Tell us what you have learned."

Peter sat down. He had rehearsed what he was going to say all the way to the hotel, but he had expected Hector to be alone.

"Maybe we should talk by ourselves," Peter suggested.

Alonzo smiled smoothly. "These men are close associates. You can speak freely in front of them."

"I found the Osbornes," he said.

Alonzo did not react. Over the past week they had heard the same thing a half dozen times from different informants, and each time the information had been wrong. Alonzo knew that if he stayed in town much longer, the Osbornes would find out that someone was making inquiries, and tell the authorities.

"How much was that reward again?" Peter asked.

"Two hundred dollars."

"I think the information I have is worth a lot more than that."

"Oh, really?"

Peter nodded. "The boy's name used to be Jack and his sister's name was Joanne."

"That is correct," Alonzo said, hiding his excitement. "What are their names now?"

"I want to talk to you about the reward money first," Peter said with a bravado he did not feel.

"I suppose we could increase it if the information you have proves to be accurate. Say . . . five hundred dollars."

Peter smiled, his confidence growing. "If you put a zero on the end of that five hundred we have a deal."

"I don't think the information is worth that much."

"I think it is, *Alonzo*."

Alonzo stared at him with astonishment. "Where did you hear that name?"

"What about the reward?"

Alonzo nodded to Paul. Paul went into the other room and came back with a thick stack bills. Alonzo laid the bills on the table in one-thousand dollar piles.

"Here's the money," Alonzo said. "But you must earn it."

Peter stared at the piles. He could go anywhere in the world with this kind of money. "They call themselves the Grangers now," he said.

Alonzo pushed a stack of bill toward Peter. Peter picked the money up.

"They live at 2276 Elm street."

Another stack was pushed over.

"His mother is opening a bookstore right across the street from here."

"Across the street," Alonzo repeated. "She was right across the street from us the whole time?" He glared at Berry and Paul.

"The store's not open yet," Peter said

"Two more to go, Peter. They are both yours if you tell me how you heard the name Alonzo."

Peter reached into his shirt pocket and took out the piece of paper he had picked up in the hallway. Alonzo stared down at the sketch. "Where did you get this?" he asked very quietly.

"It fell out of Zach's—*Jack's* journal. It's not in Jack's writing though. It must have come from someplace else."

"And where is this journal now?"

"Jack has it."

Alonzo pushed the rest of the money across, then nodded to Paul and Berry. They grabbed Peter and pinned him to the floor.

Alonzo retrieved his money. "Your information has been very valuable, Peter. Unfortunately, you know a little too

179

much for our own good."

Peter could not respond because Paul had stuffed a washrag from the bathroom into his mouth.

"What do you want to do with him?" Berry asked.

Alonzo looked down at Peter, who was still lying on the floor. "Take him to the airplane," he said. "We'll deal with him later. Tell the pilot to get the airplane ready. Berry and I will collect the other passengers and this so-called journal. The Osbornes are going on an unscheduled vacation to Colombia."

22

Sam pulled up to the Nevada Hotel after having spent the last hour driving the streets looking for Zach. He had been to his house three times and had even stopped at Darrell's to ask if he had seen Zach.

He walked up the stairs, hoping the boy had returned while he was out looking for him. Zach was not in his room. Sam stepped inside and looked around for some clue as to where he might have gone. He found Zach's backpack in the dresser, opened it, and pulled out the journal inside.

Zach was getting cold sitting outside the trailer. Where could Peter be? He hoped he wasn't out telling everyone in Elko about the Grangers being the Osbornes. If Zach didn't get back to the Nevada Hotel soon, he knew Sam would probably call the police.

That's all I need right now, he thought. If I had spoken to Catalin before dinner, I wouldn't have this problem. Who am I kidding? If I hadn't kept a journal, I wouldn't have this problem. But getting rid of the journals would have been like throwing my life away. Continuing the journal is the only thing that has kept me sane through all this.

He decided to give Peter at least another hour. The police hadn't found him walking down the busiest street in Elko and they wouldn't find him here. When he got back to the Nevada he would tell Sam that he had gone home to pick something up, stopped at Darrell's, and lost track of time.

Alonzo and Berry parked their rental car across the street from the Grangers' house.

"Doesn't look like they're home," Berry said.

"We will go inside and wait for them. Do you have your flashlight?"

The front door was locked. They went around to the back and found that door locked as well. Alonzo broke a windowpane and reached in and turned the latch. Inside, they flashed their beams around the living/dining/family room. Alonzo called Paul with his cell phone. "The Osbornes seem to have stepped out. Ask the boy where they might be."

"I'll call you back." Paul hung up.

"I'll search the bedrooms. You take the rest of the house," Alonzo ordered.

"Shouldn't take long," Berry said, looking around the tiny house.

Alonzo started in Zach's room and immediately found the journals and Jack in the Box on the bed. It didn't take him long to realize that these were old journals that were no good to him. He searched the rest of the room, without much hope of finding the journal he was looking for. The boy or his mother probably had it with them.

"In here," Berry called.

Alonzo walked out of the bedroom into the kitchen.

Berry had his flashlight beam on the phone answering machine. "You might find this interesting." He hit the play button.

"Zach, this is Mom. I was hoping we would catch you before you left. There was a mix-up with our hotel reservations. We're at the Best Western. The number is 310-555-0394, room three ninety-four. The conference is great! We're having a wonderful time. Enjoy the mountains and don't forget to take your coat. It's cold up there. We'll be home on Sunday evening. I love you."

"Thank you, Mrs. Osborne." Alonzo erased the message. He found a phone book and looked up area code 310. "We will go to Los Angeles as soon as we find the boy."

His cell phone rang. It was Paul.

"Our friend's clammed up on us. Won't say a word about where the family is."

"Fine," Alonzo said. "We're going to stop by the hotel and pick up our things and take them to the airplane. Tell Peter that if he doesn't tell you what he knows by the time I get there I will kill him."

"I'll pass it on."

Sam parked his truck across from the Grangers' and was about ready to go up to the house when he saw two men coming down the Grangers' driveway. Rather than confront them, he stayed in his cab and watched them get into a late-model car and drive away. His first thought was to follow them, but he was concerned that Zach might be in the house. As soon as their car turned the corner he grabbed the flashlight from underneath the seat and sprinted for the backyard. He found the broken windowpane. He had a good idea who these men were, or at least who they worked for. The Grangers had been discovered.

He went through the house quickly. In Zach's room he found the Jack in the Box, a pile of journals, and a tiny astronaut. On the way back to the hotel he made one more stop.

23

Cold and discouraged, Zach walked back to the Nevada Hotel. When he got there he knocked on Sam's door, and was relieved that Sam didn't answer. He went into his room and got ready for bed. There was nothing more he could do that night. He would go back to Peter's first thing in the morning and wait there all day if that's what it took. As he was getting under the covers there was a knock on the door. Zach knew who it was.

"Come in."

Sam stepped inside, closing the door behind him. "Where were you?"

"Sorry about that," Zach said. "I forgot something at home. I ran into Darrell and we started playing video games and I lost track of time."

"I went to Darrell's." Sam looked directly at him. "He hadn't seen you. Suppose you tell me what's really going on."

Sam did not seem angry, which surprised Zach. "There's nothing going on."

"You're in more trouble than you know, Zach." Sam walked over to the bed and sat down on the edge.

"Everything's fine," Zach insisted. "All I want to do is go to sleep."

Sam glanced around the room as if he was making a decision about something. He closed his eyes for a moment, then looked at Zach. "I used to have a son," he said. "When he was young I would come to his bedroom at night like this and tell him stories before he went to sleep."

"Where is he now?" Zach asked.

"He died."

"I'm sorry."

"I am, too. I'd like to tell you a story, Zach." Sam cleared his throat then began. "A long time ago there was a Russian boy who had a very good ear for music. He played the piano and everyone said that he was a musical prodigy. But he wasn't. He was just a boy who loved to listen and play music on the piano. The boy grew up, went to school, and they discovered that not only did he have a good ear for music, he also had a good ear for foreign languages. By the time he was fifteen he was fluent in five languages and he spoke those languages with perfect accents."

"You?"

Sam did not answer the question. "So, the boy gave up his music. He was sent to special schools and when he graduated they sent him to live in many different countries. On one of his trips back home he fell in love and got married. He had a son, but he did not see his son very often because he was away for long periods of time—sometimes years.

"During one of his times away his son got very ill. His wife tried to get in touch with him, but the people he worked for would not pass the message along to him. It was the policy at the time. When he finally returned home, his son had died and his wife had left him. He was filled with grief and rage and he could not be consoled. The people he worked for were very worried about him. And with good reason. During his travels, this man had learned a great deal. He carried secrets in his head that could cause immense harm to many people. He knew it was only a matter of time before someone tried to remove this threat.

"One day, the man was walking past a house with an open window. Someone inside was playing a song on the piano that he used to play when he was a child. He stood outside that window and cried. When the song ended, the man knew what he had to do. He had to share the secrets."

Sam stopped speaking. Zach stared at him wondering why he was being told this story.

"There comes a time, Zach, when you have to trust someone. I'm going to ask you again. What's going on?"

Zach trusted Sam, but if he told him who he was he was there was no hope for the Grangers staying in Elko. He didn't answer.

"How's your eyesight, Zach?"

"What do you mean?"

"It's a pretty simple question."

"My eyesight is fine."

"Why do you wear blue contacts?"

Zach looked down at the contact case on the table next to the bed.

"I'll tell you another story," Sam said. "There was a boy who came to Elko Middle School and he wasn't who he said he was. He was in the Witness Security Program and his name was Jack Osborne."

Zach gave up. "How did you know?"

"Because I read the journals in your backpack. Both of them."

Peter had his hands and feet tied and was belted into his seat. The gag had been removed and his left eye was turning black. But these were the least of his problems at the moment because Alonzo had just come aboard and taken the seat opposite him.

"I do not have a lot of time, Peter." He took a knife out of his pocket and flipped the blade open. "I need to know where Jack Osborne is. I need to know this right now."

Peter said nothing.

"You are probably thinking that I am going to kill you regardless of what you say," Alonzo continued. "You may be right about this, but there are many ways to die. I understand that you are angry . . . that I cheated you and you do not want to help me anymore."

Peter saw a movement outside the small window. A man wearing coveralls ducked under the wing. Alonzo reached over and closed the window shade. "These airplanes are soundproof," he said quietly. "I have no desire to kill you, but I will if you refuse to answer my questions. And I promise you that I will do it very slowly and it will be very painful." He put the sharp tip of the blade just below Peter's eye. Peter tried to move his head, but one of the other men came up from behind and held it steady.

"Where is Jack Osborne?" Alonzo asked.

"I don't know," Peter said hoarsely.

"I'm sorry to hear that."

Peter felt the knife tip prick his skin. Peter closed his eyes tightly and shouted, "He might be at the Nevada Hotel!"

The blade was pulled back a fraction of an inch. "Tell me more."

Peter told him everything he knew.

"You were a spy?" Zach asked, incredulous.

"We preferred to think of ourselves as intelligence officers, but at times that was an exaggeration. I was a colonel in the KGB, which is similar to your Central Intelligence Agency."

"How long have you been here?"

"I defected twenty years ago. It caused quite a stir, but of course none of this made it into your newspapers."

"Why did you defect?"

"I was tired. I did not want to work for the KGB anymore, but once you know things they don't let you leave. My only hope was to come over here and disappear. Now, let's talk about the Osbornes."

"You're not the only one who knows," Zach said. He explained the situation with Peter Short. "I went over to his trailer to try to talk him into keeping his mouth shut long enough for me to contact our handlers. I'm hoping they have a way of controlling him so we don't have to leave Elko."

"It's too late, Zach."

Sam told him about the men he saw leaving the house.

"Impossible," Zach asked. "Peter doesn't know about the men in my father's journal. *I* didn't know anything about them until I discovered Dad's journal."

"I suspect they were already in Elko looking for you when Peter found your journal. Have you seen any strangers hanging around?"

"No," Zach said. Then he remembered the man in the balcony. He told Sam about him. "We thought he was a parent."

"He could have been."

"Maybe the men you saw were thieves. Everyone in Elko knows that Mom is in Los Angeles and I'm staying at the Nevada."

Sam smiled. "The Three E's in Elko? No, I don't think so. The two men weren't carrying anything when they left your house. And by the way they tossed everything around inside, they were looking for something specific."

"They didn't find it," Zach said, glancing at the dresser. "Should I call the police?"

"Not yet. I think we should call your mother first."

"I already tried that. There must have been a mix-up with their hotel. They aren't there."

"Do you have your handlers' phone number?"

Zach shook his head.

"Do you know his name?"

"We have two. Uncle Don and Aunt Doris."

"We'll need last names."

Zach thought for a moment. "I think their names are

Doris Welty and Donald Smites, but I don't even know where they live."

"I'll find them." Sam stood up. "I still have a few friends from my old life who may be able to help. Let's go to my room."

Catalin stayed up long after her parents had gone to bed. For the past two hours she had been lying on the sofa in front of the television with the cordless phone in her hand. She had lost track of how many times she had called Sam. She tried again and this time the phone was busy. At least he's there, she thought.

Sam hung the phone up and looked at Zach. "My friend will contact your handlers."

"What about my mom and sister?"

"The Federal Marshals will find them and put them into protective custody until we get this straightened out."

"And me?"

"You're stuck with me until your handlers arrive."

"Do you have a gun?" Zach asked.

"Heavens no," Sam said. "I've never even owned a gun. Spies rarely use them. It's not like James Bond. If it had been, I would probably still be in the trade. Remember how The Phantom used traps in the novel?"

Zach nodded.

"Well, he would have been a great spy. Real spies use anticipation, guile, deceit, and they are very good at setting traps. When these fail, we run and hide, which isn't very romantic, but it works. I'm taking you up to the sheep camp where you'll be safe. While you're getting your things I'll tell Benat that we'll come back down for him tomorrow when things are clear."

Catalin redialed Sam's number. It rang and rang, but no one answered.

"I don't believe this!"

She tossed the phone onto the sofa, put her coat on, and stepped out into the cold desert night.

24

Zach sat next to Sam, clutching the backpack in his lap and trying not to think about how much trouble he and his family were in because of his mistake. They would have to start all over again. New city. New house. New names. Joanne would not play Christine. His mother would not open the bookstore. Zach might not ever see Catalin again.

"The Basques have been taking refuge in the mountains for hundreds of years," Sam said. They were about fifteen miles outside Elko and this was the first thing he had said since they pulled away from the Nevada.

Sam glanced at the backpack in Zach's lap. "I didn't tell my handler about your father's journal. I assume he's using it to make a deal."

"My dad's not making a deal!" Zach's anger flared. "He wants to get these guys as bad as anybody. I think the only reason he held it back is to make sure we were safe."

"Take a deep breath, Zach," Sam said gently. "All I'm

saying is that I think it best to keep the journal to ourselves. We'll get it to him when this is all over."

Zach was surprised at his outburst. "Sorry. I—"

Sam held his hand up. "You don't have to apologize for anything. None of this is your fault."

"How can you say that? If I hadn't kept a journal and let Peter Short get his hands on it, we would be back at the Nevada sleeping."

"It wasn't the journal that brought the men to Elko," Sam said. "They figured out the town you were in on their own. It was only a matter of time before they found out where you lived."

Zach was still not convinced. "Sounds like spy logic to me."

Sam laughed. "You may be right, we do have our own way of looking at things."

They drove a few more miles in silence, then Sam said, "I need to have you do something for me, Zach."

"Okay."

"If we get unlucky and run into these men, you have to promise me that you'll follow my lead."

"What do you mean?"

"I want you to try and stay calm. You can't think clearly if your mind is jumping all over the place. Second, I want you to do exactly as I say without question. I have been in circumstances like this more times than I care to remember and I used to be very good at it. What I'm asking is for you to trust me."

"I trust you."

Sam turned off the highway onto a dirt road.

Catalin knocked lightly on Sam's door. When there was no answer she tried Zach's door.

"Come in."

She opened the door and stepped into the dark room. The light came on. Sitting on the bed was a man dressed in black. "You must be Cat," he said. Peter had told him all about the Cristobal family.

Before she could react someone came up behind her and put a hand over her mouth. Catalin struggled, but it was no use, the man holding her was too strong.

The man on the bed took a knife out of his pocket and flipped open the blade. "Where is Zach?" he asked quietly.

The man holding her took his hand away.

"I don't know," Catalin cried hoarsely.

There was a knock at the door and the man holding her clamped his hand back over her mouth.

"Zach?" It was Benat. "Is everything all right? I thought you and Unai were going to the sheep camp."

The man on the bed smiled and said, "Bring the girl to me and open the door."

The man holding Catalin pushed her toward the bed.

Ander was standing outside the tent with a flashlight when Sam and Zach drove up. Sam walked over and explained the situation to Ander in Basque.

"How long will we stay up here?" Zach asked Sam.

"I don't know. I'll drive down to the highway late tomorrow morning and check in at the Nevada to see if your handlers have arrived."

They went into the tent where it was warm. Ander gave Zach a loaf of bread and set a wheel of cheese down on the table in front of him. Zach was not interested in eating. He listened to Ander and Sam talk in Basque for a while, then went over to one of the cots and lay down.

"That's not a bad idea," Sam said. "We should all try to get some sleep. I have some sleeping bags in the back of the truck." He came back into the tent a moment later carrying two bags and tossed one to Zach.

"I'll sleep on the floor," Zach said. There were only two cots.

"Suits me," Sam said, and unrolled his bag on the second cot.

When everyone was settled Ander turned off the Coleman lantern. Zach was exhausted, but he couldn't sleep. His mind replayed his mistakes over and over again. He was worried about his mother and sister. Were they okay? How long would it take the U.S. Marshals to find them in Los Angeles? He thought about Catalin. He missed her already. How would he feel if he had to move away and never see her again?

He listened to the men's breathing inside the tent. They seemed to have no trouble finding sleep. Unai, the shepherd. With all the other things that had happened, the news that the Elko Middle School custodian was a former Russian spy and defector seemed almost like a dream. He wondered if Sam had offered to build his mother's bookstore and have him clean out the building so he could keep a closer eye on the Grangers.

Zach closed his eyes and listened to the sheep on the hillside. After a while he fell into a fitful sleep.

* * *

"Unai?" Benat shouted from outside the tent.

Zach sat up. Sam was already on his feet. Two flashlight beams danced along the outside walls of the canvas tent like giant fireflies.

"They have Catalin," Benat said from outside. "I am sorry, but they want the boy in exchange for her."

"Send the boy out to me."

Zach recognized the voice. He had heard it in his dreams many times. "It's him," he said.

"Who?" Sam asked.

"One of the men who came to our house."

"Listen to me very carefully," the man said. "No harm will come to the girl or the old man if you do as we say."

"What do you want?" Sam asked.

"I want you to turn a light on in the tent. I will come inside and we will discuss it. And no heroics, please. Your friends will pay for any problem that you cause."

Sam whispered to Zach, "Stay calm. Follow my lead. And remember the number eight."

"What are you talking about?"

"You'll understand when the time comes."

Ander lit the Coleman lantern.

"Come on in," Sam said.

The flap opened and Benat was pushed inside, followed by a man with a ponytail holding an automatic pistol. Zach recognized him immediately from his father's sketch and he realized this was not the first time he had seen him. It was the same man he had seen in the balcony during his sister's audition, Alonzo Aznar.

Benat looked like he wanted to maul Alonzo. Ander put his hand on his shoulder and shook his head. Benat sat down on the cot and clamped his hands between his knees as if that were the only way he could stop them from tearing Alonzo apart.

"Where's Catalin?" Sam asked.

"Outside," Alonzo said. "We have done no harm to her." He looked at Zach. "So, we meet again, Jack."

Zach said nothing.

"What do you want?" Sam asked.

"Jack knows what I want," Alonzo said calmly.

Zach glanced at the backpack lying near the cot. Inside the backpack was the key to his father's cell. Outside the tent was an innocent girl who had nothing to do with this. He knew what she was going through. The confusion, the fear—all because of him. "You'll let Catalin go?" Zach asked.

"Of course," Alonzo said easily. "I have no quarrel with these people."

Zach looked at Sam.

"Let the girl go first," Sam said.

Alonzo cocked the pistol and pointed it at Sam's chest. "You are in no position to bargain."

Sam didn't appear at all concerned by the gun. In fact, he seemed somewhat amused by it, as if Alonzo were pointing nothing more dangerous than his index finger. "Let Catalin go and we'll give you what you want."

The two men stared at each other for a long time in the dim light.

"Very well," Alonzo finally said, then shouted for Catalin to be brought inside. The car door opened and a few moments later Catlin was pushed through the tent flap followed by Paul, who was also carrying a pistol. Catalin stepped over to Benat and threw her arms around him.

"We have fulfilled our part of the bargain," Alonzo said. "Now give me the journal."

Sam looked at Zach and nodded. Zach picked up his backpack and handed it to Alonzo. Alonzo opened the pack and took out a stack of opera magazines.

Alonzo took a step toward Zach. "What is this? Where is the journal?"

Zach was as surprised by the opera magazines as Alonzo was.

"He doesn't know," Sam said. "I put the magazines in there."

Alonzo pointed his pistol at Catalin. "Too bad."

Benat pushed Catalin behind him.

"If you kill anyone in this tent," Sam told him quietly, "you will never get the journal and I guarantee you that it will find its way to the police."

"Who are you?" Alonzo asked.

"I'm a school custodian."

Alonzo scoffed. "You do not act like a custodian."

Once again the two men stared at each other. The silence was broken by Alonzo. "We are wasting time, Mr. Custodian."

"I agree," Sam said. "Let's you and me and your friend drive back to Elko and get the journal."

"The boy will come with us."

"No," Sam said.

"I'll go." Zach wasn't about to let Sam go off with these men alone.

"It's not necessary, Zach."

"On the contrary, Mr. Custodian." Alonzo leveled his pistol at Zach's head. "I insist."

25

As they left the tent Catalin covered her face and began sobbing. Sam told her not to worry, that everything would be fine. Zach wished he had just a little of Sam's confidence.

Outside, Alonzo turned to Paul. "Did you disable their truck?"

"They aren't going anywhere unless they walk. I also opened the corral and scattered the horses."

"Very good. After you, gentlemen."

They rode down the Ruby Mountains in complete silence. Zach was in the front seat with Paul. Sam in the backseat with Alonzo. Zach spent his time trying to figure out why Sam wanted him to remember the number eight. After his initial surprise at the men showing up at the camp, Sam had been as calm as Zach had ever seen him. It was almost as if Sam were the one in control, not Alonzo. He must have devised a way to get out of this, but Zach had no idea what it might be. When they got to Elko, Alonzo asked Sam where to go.

"Elko Middle School," Sam said. "The journal is in my workshop."

Paul parked in front of the school. "You stay with the boy," Alonzo said. "I will go inside with the custodian to get the journal."

"No," Sam insisted. "Zach stays with me or you're not getting the journal."

After some thought Alonzo relented. "Very well, we will all go inside, but I am warning you. If you try anything, the boy will be killed."

Sam nodded. "I understand."

They got out of the car and walked up the stairs to the school.

Sam unhooked the ring of keys on his belt and found the right one for the front door.

"Is there an alarm?" Alonzo asked.

"Yes."

"And you know the code to turn it off?"

"Of course."

"I hope so," Alonzo said. "Because if an alarm goes off, silent or otherwise, and the police come here, Zach will—"

"We understand," Sam interrupted. "You'll get your journal. We won't spring any traps on you."

Zach looked at Sam. *Spies are very good at setting traps.* Sam was trying to tell him something. He led them down the hallway and opened the office door. Inside, near the receptionist's desk was a keypad with a red blinking light. Alonzo shone his flashlight on it and Sam quickly entered the code. The light turned to green. "We're all set."

"Keep ahold of the boy," Alonzo said to Paul, taking a position a few feet behind Sam.

Paul grabbed Zach's arm and they followed Alonzo and Sam down the dark hallway. Alonzo's and Paul's cowboy boots clacked eerily on the old linoleum as they made their way to the auditorium. Zach was still surprised at how calm Sam appeared. He acted as if he were escorting a couple of teachers to the auditorium, not two men holding guns. Zach was anything but calm. His hand had gone numb from Paul's pinching his biceps so tightly; his legs felt like mud; and his heart was slamming in his chest like a wild bird trapped in a cage. He was certain that Alonzo was going to kill them as soon as he had the journal. He remembered exactly what Alonzo had said to his mother before he left their home that night. *We are very serious men. If you call the police or tell anyone about what happened this evening we will come back and kill you and your children.* They had gone to the police. They had broken his trust. Zach had told Sam all of this at the Nevada, but he didn't think Sam understood how dangerous Alonzo was.

Sam pulled open the door of the pitch-black auditorium. Alonzo shone his flashlight around the inside, which did little to illuminate the dark cavern.

"Are there windows?" he asked.

"No," Sam said.

"Then turn on all of the lights."

"No problem." Sam stepped inside and opened a small metal panel built into the wall. He switched on the lights one by one, including the house lights. Zach looked at the stage and noticed that several of the props had been moved since he was last there. The punching bag had been dragged to the center of the stage.

Alonzo turned his flashlight off and carefully scanned the auditorium. When he was satisfied there was no one waiting in the shadows for him, he turned to Sam. "Where is your room?"

"Beneath the stage."

They walked down the center aisle to the small door near the stage, which was only wide enough for them to pass through one at a time. When they reached the end of the short corridor, Sam unlocked his door and turned on the workroom light.

Zach looked around. Sam had dragged his recliner to the center of the large room. On the seat was his Jack in the Box.

"Where is the journal?" Alonzo asked.

"I'll get it," Sam said, and started toward the recliner.

Zach stared at the box in surprise. There was something different about it.

"Stop," Alonzo ordered.

Sam did as he was told.

"I will get the journal." Alonzo looked at Paul. "Cover them."

Paul pushed Zach against the workbench and waved Sam over with his gun.

"You'll need a key," Sam said. He unclipped the key holder from his belt.

Zach suddenly realized what was different about the box. The padlock had a big red eight on it. Sam had set a trap. Above the door in the ceiling was something heavy.

He had created an upside-down Jack in the Box. *Real spies use anticipation, guile, and deceit.* Spies also have a sense of humor, Zach thought, forcing himself not to look up at the ceiling and give the trap away.

Sam took his time going through the keys.

"Hurry up!" Alonzo said.

"Sorry, they all look alike."

Zach knew that Sam was giving him time to figure out how to spring the trap. He turned his head and looked at the levers above the bench. Casually, he put his hand on the bench beneath the row of levers.

"Here it is," Sam said, taking it off the ring.

Alonzo stepped over to him and took the key. "The journal had better be inside."

"You have my word." Sam glanced over at Zach. "I'm sorry about this, Zach. I know you wanted to keep the journal for your Dad, but sometimes things just don't work out as we anticipate."

"That's okay," Zach said. He would have to time the pull perfectly.

Alonzo walked over to the recliner and looked down at the box. He opened the lock and took it out of the hasp. He opened the box.

"What is this?" Alonzo shouted in rage. He reached into the box and came out with Commander IF in his hand.

Zach pulled the lever.

The punching bag crashed down on Alonzo. At the same moment, Sam grabbed Paul's arm and swung him against the wall. A shot went off and splintered the ceiling. Sam slammed Paul's gun hand against the workbench and the pistol went skidding across the floor. Zach dove for it. By the time he got back to his feet, Sam had Paul under control.

"We need to tie him up," he said.

Zach found just the thing for the job. He found a roll of duct tape and proceeded to bind Paul's hands and feet. When he was finished, he walked over to the unconscious Alonzo Aznar. Commander IF was lying next to him. Zach put his imaginary friend in his pocket and walked away.

Uncle Don arrived at the school accompanied by several U.S. Marshals. Alonzo was conscious now and tied up like Paul with duct tape. Uncle Don walked over to him and read him his rights, then joined Zach and Sam, who were sitting on the workbench.

"Hello, Zach."

"I slipped up," Zach said.

"I know. We found a kid named Peter Short on Alonzo's jet. He told us all about it. We also found Alonzo's other man and his new pilot. They're in custody."

"What about my mom and sister?"

"We found them too. Doris is on her way to Los Angeles. They're fine, but not too happy about all this."

"What's going to happen now?"

"Well, it looks like the Grangers are moving out of Elko immediately."

"But we have Alonzo." Zach felt his hope slipping away.

"I see that," Uncle Don said. "Unfortunately, he can still get to you from jail. Money has a long reach. I'm taking you out of here. We're going to meet your mom and sister and start this all over again."

Zach knew Uncle Don was right. This would never be over.

"The kid in the airplane said something about a journal belonging to your father. Do you know anything about that?"

Zach shook his head. "Nope."

Uncle Don stared at him for a moment. "Well, the kid wasn't making much sense. He was pretty scared."

Zach glanced down into his shirt pocket. You're getting better at this, Commander IF said. Zach smiled. "Before we go I want to talk to Sam alone."

"Go ahead. But make it quick. I have an airplane waiting for us at the airport. Your mom and sister are already en route."

Zach knew better than to ask where they were heading. He and Sam walked up to the stage and sat on the piano bench. They spent a few moments watching the men and women moving around the workshop through the trapdoors.

"Thanks, Sam."

"To tell you the truth, Zach, it was kind of fun. It reminded me of the old days."

"Will you tell Catalin what happened? She deserves an explanation."

"I'll tell her."

"And what about the journal?"

"It's safe," Sam assured him. "I can give it to you before you go, but it might be best to let me get it to your dad."

"How?"

"It's better that you don't know. Spies have their own way of doing things."

Zach nodded. He knew Sam would get the journal to his father.

"You're in as much trouble as I am, now. Alonzo's not going to forget what you did. I bet they would put you into the protection program if you asked."

Sam shook his head. "I spent most of my life pretending to be someone I wasn't. Besides, I have an opera to put on. No, I'm going to stay right here. If Alonzo comes after me, I think I have enough guile left in me to deal with the situation." He put his arm around Zach's shoulders. "A shepherd stays with his flock."

26

Dear Catalin,

I'm sorry it has taken me so long to write this letter. . . .

They wouldn't allow me to write to you until just before we were ready to leave here, and to be honest, I didn't know what to say—"Sorry I almost got you and your grandfather killed. . . ." sounded a little shallow. Another reason is that my handlers wouldn't let me write this at all unless I agreed to let them read the letter before they sent it. I can't blame them, since my writing got everyone into quite a bit of trouble in Elko. So, I hope you'll understand if I can't say everything in this letter that I want to.

Soon, we'll be leaving for our new home. We are no longer the Grangers and I'm no longer called Zach. We are looking forward to getting out of here and starting our lives over again. My sister is still irritated with me for screwing up her chance to star in The Opera Ghost. Hopefully she'll get over it soon. My mom has been great through this whole thing despite losing her bookstore.

I think of Benat and the Ruby Mountains every day and wish I was back up there with you. I also wish that I could write to you every day, but this will be my last letter. Someday I would like to come back to Elko and see you.

Love, Zach

Zach put his pencil down and read the letter over. He was still dissatisfied. Commander IF stood on the desk near the sheet of paper. It's your last chance, he said.

"I know," Zach said.

Zach picked up his pencil again.

P.S. I wish I could slip into this envelope and send myself to you. I can't, so I've sent Commander IF in my place. He's been a good friend to me and I'm sure he'll be a good friend to you.

He gave the letter to Aunt Doris and watched as she read it. When she finished she folded it and put it into an envelope along with Commander IF.

"I don't see any problems, Mack," she said. "I'll mail it when I get back home."

Mack Greene. Short for Mackenzie. They said he could choose his own name this time. "Why can't you mail it now?" he asked. "We're leaving this afternoon."

"A precaution," Aunt Doris said. "We don't want anyone picking up your trail here."

His sister came out of the bedroom with her bag. Her hair had grown out a little and was back to its original color. She looked a lot more like his sister now. She had chosen Christine for her new name. "The private jet will make it

210

easier this time," Uncle Don said.

The jet had belonged to Alonzo Aznar. It had been "arrested" and was serving its time by flying witnesses to their new homes.

"Mom will be there?" Christine asked.

"Yep. She boarded two hours ago."

Mrs. Greene had been spending a lot of time with the DEA, testifying against Alonzo Aznar.

Mack and Christine were taken to a private airfield. The small jet made a perfect landing and taxied over to where they were waiting. The door opened and the stairs were lowered.

"Welcome aboard," Mrs. Greene said with a smile.

Mack and Christine looked at each other in surprise. They hadn't seen her this happy in a very long time. They climbed the stairs.

As soon as they found their seats the jet began to taxi out to the runway and a voice came over the intercom, "This is Captain Brennan. Our flying time today will be approximately two hours."

Mack still didn't know where they were going. In two hours they could be just about anywhere.

"My co-pilot today is Robert. . . . Well, I think I'll let him introduce himself."

The cockpit door opened and the co-pilot stepped out. He was a thin man with blond hair and tired blue eyes. Mack and Christine jumped out of their seats and ran to him. He looked a lot like their father. His name was Robert Greene.

Acknowledgments

Thanks again to my faithful and astute readers: Bethany Culpepper, Melanie Gill, Mike Scrivens, Brenda Roydon, and my fabulous wife, Marie, who keeps me out of trouble. A special thanks to Sam Sebesta, a hero in his own right, for letting me use his name for my hero.

Roland Smith enjoys hearing from his readers. You can contact him by accessing his Web page at **www.rolandsmith.com** or by writing to him at P.O. Box 911, Tualatin, OR 97062.